Never A Dull Moment

Never A Dull Moment

✦

You'll experience a whole new way to look at the underworld.

Berardino M D'Angelo

iUniverse, Inc.
New York Lincoln Shanghai

Never A Dull Moment

You'll experience a whole new way to look at the underworld.

iUniverse books may be ordered through booksellers or by contacting:

iUniverse
2021 Pine Lake Road, Suite 100
Lincoln, NE 68512
www.iuniverse.com
1-800-Authors (1-800-288-4677)

ISBN-13: 978-0-595-39485-2 (pbk)
ISBN-13: 978-0-595-83882-0 (ebk)
ISBN-10: 0-595-39485-X (pbk)
ISBN-10: 0-595-83882-0 (ebk)

Printed in the United States of America

Contents

Part II

Part III

Part IV

Acknowledgments

Gloria D'Angelo
Bernie D'Angelo, Jr.
Beth D'Angelo
Vincent D'Angelo
Jimmy D'Angelo, Jr.
Linda D'Angelo
Gerry D'Angelo
Kathy Mitros D'Angelo
Tony D'Angelo
Pat D'Angelo Rillera
Rebecca Griswold
Scott Griswold
Julie Griswold
Peter Cordua
Barbara Henwood
Danny Cordua
Walter Gimpel
Linda Gimpel
Catherine Gimpel
Dr. Jack McGovern
Marion McGovern
Bill King
Bunny King
Robin Rillera West
Diane Rillera
Bob Moseson
Janis Moseson
Jamie Gayle
Sean Clancy
Eric Tucker

Carl Schmollinger
Gloria Schmollinger

Special thanks to Mary and Jim for the fun!

Although this book is about Jim, he had colorful cohorts, friends, and relatives who were surprisingly unpredictable and interesting. The women characters in this book (my mother, aunts, friends, and so on) are strong and as equally unpredictable as the mobsters themselves. *Never a Dull Moment* will keep you turning the pages with great anticipation. You'll experience a whole new way to look at the underworld.

Background

Most people sometime in their lives have a hero, often a sports figure or a movie star or the like; mine was and still is my old man. His appeal did not stop with me or with the immediate members of my family. Most everyone that met him fell under the spell. It was uncanny the way he could win over people from all walks of life, social standings, and income brackets; not even Ripley would believe it. Jimmy D'Angelo, aka the Cisco Kid, led an exotic fun-filled life to say the least. He made his living hustling and dealt with everyone from the mob to the clergy, and he was held in high esteem by both. However, unlike the mob guys, he wasn't violent; he lived to steal and stole to live while accumulating more followers than the pope.

My mother was an Irish Catholic, and for forty years she tried to reform my dad through prayers, novenas, the lighting of candles, and anything else she could think of to reform him, but the efforts didn't make a dent. However, she appreciated him and the exciting life they had together. My mother's name is Mary; together they were like real-life "Honeymooners" à la the Jackie Gleason show (and my father even resembled Jackie Gleason in appearance). My father said they'd been fighting for forty years, and he never once won, not even a draw.

I looked at my dad like a modern-day Robin Hood who stole from the greedy and shared with the needy, but kept a large chunk for himself. After all, he was Robin Hood, not Mother Teresa, and he was the brains behind everything in which he was involved. In the early days he lived in a poor, blue-collar neighborhood, and he was king—and for a good reason. The people were needy, and Jim filled their needs. They lived on budgets and very rarely ate high on the hog, except for when Jim would acquire a truckload of lobster or beef. And then the price was right, and it was surf and turf for the whole neighborhood. The rest went to local butchers and markets at way-below-wholesale. When everyone in the neighborhood was riding around on new rubber and local gas stations were having tire sales, you knew that Jim was at it again. Jim from time to time would brag that he had fifty arrests and no convictions. The claim about fifty arrests was correct, but the no-convictions part was not exactly true.

1

PART I

The Still

When I was about five, Dad had a rather large still in the Richmond section of Philadelphia. One day, my dad, my grandfather, and I went for a ride, stopping at Dad's furniture-refinishing shop, which was in a large warehouse that also housed Dad's still. My father went inside, leaving my grandfather and me in the car. Moments later, undercover agents came out with my father and about six of his cohorts. The agent opened the car door and grabbed my grandfather, who did not know what was going on and was completely innocent. He just happened to be at the wrong place at the wrong time. He was an honest shoemaker; it was a case of locking up the piano player when raiding the whorehouse. My grandfather was so mad that he took a swing at Jim. Jim ducked, and my grandfather decked the cop; he was swearing in Italian with two undercover agents holding him. He was biting his fists and looking at Jim with fire in his eyes (biting your fists in any language or culture is not a sign of affection). Usually my grandfather was a happy, cute old man who reminded me of Santa Claus, but this was not one of those times. By some miracle the agents let my grandfather and me go. My grandfather went home, and I went with him. Somehow my father got away with just probation. The still was shut down, but my father continued to run his shop out of the warehouse where he refinished and reupholstered furniture for local Philadelphia furniture and department stores such as John Wanamaker's, JB Van Sciver, Strawbridge's, and many other fine furniture galleries. He had as many as forty employees and also had twelve racehorses. He paid his employees well, and things ran smoothly. He was very generous with his family and friends, and he thought it was his responsibility to help anyone who needed it. This kept him working and hustling.

The Shot

My father had a dice table that he had specially made for something he called "the shot." With the shot, he could take a legitimate set of dice and throw any number he desired; it was like magic. This was a skill that few people possessed, and he was the best. When the mob had Las Vegas nights, clambakes, or a game they called "Jim" or whenever and wherever else gamblers gathered, Jim and his magic table were there. Over the years he won fortunes while mesmerizing gamblers, even though they were losing a bundle. When he would practice his skill, like a baseball player practices pitches, he would throw as many as fifty straight numbers. He mastered cards as well. He could deal off the bottom, false shuffle, and "move coolers" ("move coolers" means to change decks without anyone seeing). The new deck was pre-stacked and everyone would have a great hand, but Jim would have the winning hand. He would bring the cooler deck into the game by slight of hand and misdirection. It would be the same brand and color as the original deck. When the switch was made, the old deck would disappear, and the new deck would appear. The move would be made after someone was asked to cut the cards; again it was like magic.

When it came to gambling, Jim was loaded for bear. He had all the tools to do the job; no job was too big and no job was too small. He loved the action and would gamble for days at a time without sleep. His shills would line up customers. At one game, he had out-of-town businessmen whom he had lured to the game by hiring hookers. One of the hookers, a black woman, said to my father, "I'ze not a hooker; I'ze an eggs-ziotic dancer."

Jim said to her, "If you don't get your eggs-ziotic ass out there, you're not getting paid." Needless to say, she got paid and paid well. She told Jim to call if he ever needed her again, and she gave him several numbers where she could be reached.

When the game started, Jim kept the energy level at a fevered pitch with his underworld wit, jokes, and one-liners. The "marks" (customers) left happier than when they had come, having had a subcultural experience of fun and games not found in Disneyland or almost any other place on the earth. The marks would comment on how much they enjoyed themselves, and they couldn't wait for the next time Jim would have a game. Jim, being master of human nature, would play hard-to-get. They actually would give Jim their names and numbers, and that was like giving Dracula the keys to the blood bank. As soon as the marks left, Jim and his shills would chop up the cash, and the shills could not wait for the next game either.

The shills were paid well and looked at Jim like puppies, not knowing Jim had already devised a scheme to get back some of the money he paid them. Jim said that if you let them keep all the money, they would get lazy and not want to work when needed. You might ask how he would go about getting back money from the shills without their realizing they had been hustled. After all, the shills were hustlers too. Well, there are doctors, and there are specialists—and Jim was a specialist. Like a fine surgeon, he could sever the ties between them and their money without their feeling a thing. You may have heard the saying "you can't cheat an honest man," but these weren't honest men. If they were gamblers, he'd go in that direction and use that to his advantage; if they were greedy, he'd go in that direction; and if they were greedy gamblers, it was a piece of cake.

You Can't Cheat an Honest Man

I mentioned earlier that Jim had racehorses. You've probably heard of fixing a horse race to make a winner. Well it's easier to make a loser. I'll explain. Jim would let news slip out that one of his horses was running, and he was going to give him the stuff. This was a miracle potion that would make the horse run faster, like a track star on steroids. If he were already a favorite, the stuff would be the edge—or like the shills would say, a "sure thing." But as you know, the only thing sure is that good girls go to heaven and bad girls go everywhere (I just thought that was cuter than death and taxes.). Now that the shills thought they had an edge, considering that the horse did win from time to time and that the odds were two or three to one, Jim could convince them that with the stuff the horse would win easily.

However, the opposite was going to happen: Jim gave the order to the jockey to "pull him" (which means to hold him back and make him lose). This would go by undetected. The information that the horse was running would reach the shills close to post time, the start of the race. This left no time for them to get to the track. Jim knew that they would bet with the local bookie, and combined, they would bet a considerable amount of money. In the meantime, Jim had called the bookie to tell him that he was stiffing the horse and that he should expect these guys to come in and bet a bundle and should take their "action" (bets). The bookie, knowing that the horse was going to lose, would be glad to do this and give half the bets he received to Jim. After all, there was no gambling involved. I guess it was indeed a sure thing—for Jim and the bookie anyway. Jim would also instruct the bookie to leak that Jim too had bet a bundle on this horse. Then, after the horse would lose, the shills would think everybody took a bath.

People would want to know what happened to the sure thing. Jim would tell everyone that the horse sustained an injury, a tendon or ankle injury, for example, leaving everyone to believe that it was just one of those things that happen. Running the horse in the race even though he didn't win gave the horse great conditioning and exercise, and having him lose also would drive the odds up the next time he would run. Now the next time he would run, the odds would be five to one, instead of two or three to one. Because the story was out that he was coming off an injury, no one would bet him. But Jim was going to bet him, and this time he would tell the jockey to put the pedal to the metal, also telling the jockey that there was a sizeable bet on the horse for him. This ensured that the jockey would do his best to get the horse to the wire. When the horse would win, Jim would collect the purse and the bets, and the scene was set for his next adventure. Jim had more twists than a twenty-foot boa.

Mary Challenges Jim's Gambling

My mother, Mary, and father, Jim, had been married for about eight years or so, and my father was always away gambling or doing whatever he does. He had been doing this since day one, and now my mother was angry and was going to teach him a lesson. So she sold all the furniture in the house and put the money in the middle of the dining room floor. When Jim came home, she told him, "You love gambling so much—take the money and get out." She had sold the furniture to several different people.

Jim took this mild setback and turned it into a triumph. He asked around the neighborhood and found out who bought the bedroom set and went to the woman and told her this: "I know you got a great buy, and I wouldn't blame you if you wouldn't sell it back to me, but you see, my wife does this often, selling things and other bizarre behavior. You see, she's mentally unbalanced and should be in a hospital, but I love her too much to do that." (This, of course, was grade-A bullshit.)

The woman said, "You poor man, I will sell it back to you. I know the other people that bought the rest, and I will go with you to get it." And when the other women heard his story, their hearts went out to him. Knowing human nature, he told them, "Because of the things she does, I'm a little short on money." He not only bought the furniture back, but even got it for less than the buyers had paid. Jim had struck again. My mother never knew how he did it till several months later when she found out from a neighbor the story he had told those women. That night, never saying anything to him, she waited till he went to bed. While he was sleeping, she sat straddled over his arms and chest and beat him over the head with a mop handle. Jim woke up, but it took him a few seconds to shake loose and to grab his clothes and shoes while Mom was getting in a few more licks. He ran out of the house and down the alley to make his getaway. The rumors you hear about the Irish being quick-tempered and ready to fight are not rumors; when my mother got her Irish up, somebody was going to get their ass kicked, and this time it was Jim.

Uncle Sal's Favorite Story (Mary and Charlie the Cab Driver)

My father's brother, my uncle Sal, told me this story. It was one of his favorites. (By the way, Jim had three brothers and a sister, the oldest brother Alex, then Barney, then Jim, then Sal, and a sister, Camille. I'm not sure where Camille fits in the age category; I may be brave, but I am not going there). Alex was also in the furniture business. Barney was in show business, a stand-up comic. Sal was a musician, a writer of songs and comedy. Camille, who was called Meelie, was a mother and a homemaker. The story that Sal told me took place when we lived next door to a firehouse in Philadelphia at 2071 East Clearfield Street. I know this story to be true because I remember it, and you will soon see why.

I was about six. There were two apartments; we lived on the first floor, and Charlie and Mary Moller lived on the second floor. Sal had stopped by to talk to my dad, and my mother told him to sit down because my father would be home in a few minutes. Charlie, who lived upstairs, was a cabdriver and was gone most of the day and night working. Mary got lonely from time to time, and she would have male visitors. If memory serves me, Mary was blond, pretty, built, and had a gentle nature. I guess you could say she was "giving." One Saturday afternoon, when Mary had a visitor, Charlie made an unscheduled stop home. He parked his cab and went upstairs. I wanted to warn her; even though I was only six, I knew the shit was about to hit the fan. Just the opposite of Mary, Charlie was nasty, less than intelligent, and drunk most of the time. This day he had had a few. Yes, he was a drunken cabby. When he got upstairs, I heard screams, shuffling, and cursing. Then the male visitor came running down the steps with clothes in hand, naked as a newborn. Then Mary came down naked too, but with no clothes in hand. Then Charlie came down fully clothed, gun in hand.

The naked visitor vanished into the street, but Mary could only get about thirty feet from the door, clutching a telephone pole to protect herself and to cover her from onlookers and doing a bad job of both. And Charlie, raising the gun in a drunken, jealous rage shouted, "I'm gonna blow your fuckin whore brains out!" By this time, the firemen next door were watching, along with neighbors and passersby, but no one would help; they just froze. From out of nowhere, Jim stepped between Mary and Charlie. Now the gun was pointed at Jim. Talking softly, but with authority, he agreed with Charlie that she was a no-good whore and so were all women. As he got closer, I couldn't hear every word, but he got Charlie's confidence. He took the gun and sat him down on the stoop and stayed with him till the cops came. Jim helped put Charlie in the wagon. The onlookers wanted to praise him, but he just smiled and walked into the house, said, "When's dinner?" to my mother, and made no more out of it. The neighborhood buzzed the story for weeks, but Jim was already focused on other things.

A short time later, Charlie got out of jail and went home to get his clothes. My parents were there to make the peace. Somehow they got these crazies to make up, but down the road Mary and Charlie broke up for good.

Tony's Christening

While we were still living next to the firehouse, a man in an army jeep came to visit my sister, Patsy. She was two years older than I was. The man was my mother's first husband and Patsy's father, Joe Sheckler. He was a big six-foot-plus, two-hundred-pound-plus, ex-heavyweight fighter and paratrooper and one nice guy. He was always as good to me as he was to my sister and a good, close friend of my dad. It would seem odd, especially for the time, but the personality of Jim, or Jimmy D., as he was also known, would even appeal to an ex. Later in life, I would become a professional fighter, and Joe would become my first trainer.

At that time, Joe was a detective for the railroad; that automatically put Jim in the business of emptying boxcars. It seemed that whatever people needed, Jim had it: cars, boats, loans, lawyers, things for the home, and even connections to get your kid into a good college or job. The list went on.

I mentioned my sister Patsy, the oldest; then came me, and then there were my brothers, Jimmy, Gerry, and Tony. Tony was born when my mother was in her forties, which surprised us kids. We never thought they were still playing "hide the salami." At that time, we were living in a colonial mansion on Roosevelt Boulevard in the far northeast section of Philadelphia. I think my dad thought he was Elvis—because the house looked suspiciously like Graceland.

Dad had a christening for Tony that was like something out of *The Godfather*, with caterers, singers, comedians, dancers, a full orchestra, and about five hundred close friends—a mix of gangsters, politicians, priests, and nuns, rich and poor, old and young—and it was a blast. I was sixteen, and there was more food, booze, women, and just plain excitement than I'd ever seen! My mother felt like a queen, and she looked the part; Mom always had style, stature, and class as long as you didn't piss her off.

Cops, on and off duty, were there; Jim was not a novice at throwing parties. It was a good thing the cops were there because in the height of the festivities, a fight broke out in the driveway alongside the house. I went out to see what was happening as my father was helping his friend Tony Martino up off the ground. Tony, naturally, had one of those extra-large Italian "snot lockers." It was evident that he had just eaten a knuckle sandwich, and the guy who had hit him was still mouthing insults. I remember they called him "Shieldsy"; he was fresh out of prison and had a chip on his shoulder.

Jimmy D. approached Shieldsy and politely asked him to leave. Shieldsy hurled an insult at him, along with another knuckle sandwich—this time without success. Jim moved slightly out of the way and threw a straight right hand, which he called "the Maryann." Maryann broke Shieldsy's upper jaw, taking out most of his front teeth. Shieldsy didn't wake up till halfway to the hospital, and then he vowed he would never do anything like that again. After all, how many of those hits can you take?

The party continued on into the night. All in all, it was a memorable event.

Photo of Fuente wearing # 7—people in photo from left to right Jimmy
D'Angelo, Berardino D'Angelo, and trainer Dave Ginsburg.

Fuente's Birthday Party

While we're on the topic of parties, Jim owned a winning racehorse named "Fuente." For the horse's birthday, he rented a hall, a band, and caterers—the works. He had the horse walking around the hall with a guy dressed like a jockey, with a broom and shovel to clean up after the horse (just in case). The man who owned the hall, Mr. DePinto, saw the horse and went nuts, screaming, hollering, and jumping up and down. Jim put his hand in his pocket and gave him a fistful of hundreds. Mr. DePinto smiled and wished the horse a happy birthday. Fuente was extremely docile and calm for a thoroughbred, and he left the party early. After all, an athlete needs his sleep. This particular horse was like a puppy. If you walked around, he would follow. If you ran and played, he would also. He would lean his head against you and liked to be petted.

How Jim got Fuente is a story in itself. Jim's horse trainer, Dave Ginsberg (the salt of the earth), called him and said there was a four-year-old that was going to be put down. Even though the horse hadn't won in two years and most race-horses are over the hill at that age, Dave said the horse had heart and asked if he could bring him around. My dad knew how much Dave loved horses, and we knew how much Jim loved Dave, and my mother said to Jim, "If you don't buy this horse, you greedy Dago bastard, you're going to burn in hell." Well, with all that sentiment, how could he not? He bought Fuente for the money it took to transport him to the stable where Dave could work on him. Dave was also broke and not winning when Jim hired him, and I can tell you where Dave lived: he lived in a tack room at the track. A tack room is where they keep saddles, bridles and other things used on the horses. He had a cot and a small coal oil heater that he used to keep warm, to cook, and to make coffee. Maybe that's why Dave had empathy for Fuente.

Anyway, hiring Dave turned out great. Although Jim thought that buying Fuente was just a matter of buying another hay burner and that he was just doing it to make his buddy happy, he couldn't have been more wrong. In three months Fuente started to race. Fuente never looked like a muscled-up thoroughbred; he was built more like a plow horse than a racehorse. He looked like a Clydesdale! However, Dave was right. He got him healthy, and with Fuente's big heart he started winning. He had more wins than all the other horses my father owned combined. Fuente always seemed to be in the money. He was a gold mine and loved to race. Wouldn't you give him a party?

Photo of Fuente wearing #4—people in photo from right to left Dave
Ginsburg, Mary D'Angelo, and Jimmy D'Angelo.

Mom Whips the Jockey

My mother loved Fuente, and when he'd race, she would tell the jockey not to use his whip on him. "If he wants to slow up, you let him," she said, and she told the jockey not to even carry the whip.

Jim stepped in and said, "Mary, the other guys will laugh at him and call him sissy."

So Mom agreed that he could carry it, but ordered, "Don't use it!" Jim assured her that the jockey wouldn't. Jim gave the jockey the eye, and the jockey knew what to do. When the race started, he came out of the gate, and the jocks were yelling and whipping—and so was our jock. Jim had earlier instructed the jock to "ride to win," and this meant using the whip when needed. Fuente won. When the group gathered in the winner's circle, where the jock, the horse, the owners, and the trainer got their picture taken, Mom, instead of posing for the picture, pulled the jock off the horse and took his whip from him. She started to whip the jockey, screaming, "How do you like it, you little bastard!" Then she went after Jim, who was laughing so hard that he could barely defend himself. Mom was ordered off the track for conduct unbecoming a sportsman, but Mom told the stewards (the governing body) to blow it out their ass and told Jim that if it happened again, she would take the whip and shove it up his dago ass. When Mom got her Irish up, she meant business.

Jim Goes Broke

Jim and Mary lived high those years, as did we children. But being the risk taker that he was, Jim went up and down several times in his life. One time he hit bottom (he was broke or close to it), and he told my mother not to use her credit cards. As he put it, things were tough. My mother had heard this before and paid it no mind. She thought he was trying to control her spending, and Mom didn't like to be controlled, so she did the opposite of what he ordered. She went shopping at John Wanamaker's and made several purchases. The salesperson rang it up and told her that her charge card was invalid. She hit the roof, screaming and yelling and vowing to kill Jim when he got home. When she got home, she went after Jim telling him as she threw punches how humiliated she was. Jim backed away and said, "I told you we don't have any M-O-N-F-E-Y," spelling out the letters.

Hearing this, my mother said, "You stupid dago, there is no 'F' in money."

Jim replied, "That's what I've been trying to tell you." It took the whole family to restrain her so that Jim could make his getaway and keep her from the cutlery drawer. Now she was up to "carving him in small pieces." Jim was broke but would rise again.

Giving the Horse His Vitamins

Back when Jim had horses, I lived at the racetrack. I worked mucking out stalls (that's racetrack jargon for cleaning up horseshit). I also learned to ride during that time. Jim was excited that he would have a jockey in the family who would win and lose on command. However, his dream was short-lived because nature took over, and I got too big and too heavy. Jimmy D. was crushed, but he got over it. Instead of riding, I helped give horses their vitamins (juice, or "the stuff") because the track cops were used to seeing me go in and out of the stalls.

One time, one of Jim's geniuses mixed the stuff a little too strong, and Jim gave a horse named Nate Hershfield a little too many vitamins. Nate won the third race and then was still running by the time they tried to start the fourth race. The horse had run all over the track and jumped over the infield railing. Halfway over the railing, he lost the jockey and began running around the infield, having a ball. He was finally cornered (uninjured) and taken back to the shed row (the stable). I had to walk Nate till he cooled down, which took about thirty minutes, and then wash him with a hose. The horse loved it. Nate was a new edition to the stable and the fact that the horse circled the track a couple a hundred of times and had to be chased down and brought back to the stable area did not bother Jim one iota. The only thing he cared about was that Nate was a winner, and in Jim's book, that made him a keeper; Nate was a welcome addition to the club of eight horses.

Photo of August Bull—people in picture from left to right Jimmy
D'Angelo, Mary D'Angelo, and Lenny Basile.

Lenny the Barber, Vince, and Nicky

I want to tell you how Jim got his first horse. It was about 1956 when he entered into half-ownership of a horse named August Bull. The horse had been owned by a mailman and a barber, and the mailman sold his half to Jim. The barber, a colorful character by the name of Lenny Basil, became Jim's partner. Lenny's barbershop was located in a place in northeastern Philadelphia called the Northeast Village. This was low-rent housing for servicemen after World War II. Although it was temporary housing, it was up for about twelve years. The houses were built like army barracks, and the roads had names like Midway, Wake, Atol, and Beachhead. It was like a little city to itself. There was a supermarket, a drugstore, a community building, a gymnasium, and a library. Outside there were football fields, baseball fields, and areas for volleyball and basketball. Even though no one had much, there were good neighbors, a lot of activities for the kids, and no pretense among the adults. They were all ex-servicemen and women and seemed to have a lot in common.

One thing that the community members had in common was that everyone went to Lenny's barbershop, men and women alike. It was not uncommon for people to go to the barbershop and find the shades pulled down with a sign on the door that read, "Be back in an hour." This meant that the barber was getting a little "trim". Lenny was quite the ladies man. The whole village knew what he was up to, and yet he somehow never got caught by an irate husband. When he became Jimmy D'Angelo's partner in August Bull, he was in for even more thrills.

Jim made Lenny his private gigolo and told Lenny that rich women need love too. Jim liked to turn everything into a moneymaker. Jim and Lenny would take a rich woman for a day at the track. Lenny would flatter and romance her while Jim would study the race sheet and look for losers. Jim would claim to have a tip on one of the dogs he had picked and say that he was going to the window to bet a thousand. Lenny would say, "Here's a thousand for me." Then the woman, wanting to be a part of it, would give Jim a thousand for her. They would make sure that there was a minute or less time left before the start of the race. So Jim would have to hurry. Jim would run up to the window but would not buy any tickets. He would stay there till the race was over and then pick up discarded tickets off the floor. By this time, Lenny and the woman, having watched the race, would know that the horse that they supposedly bet on lost. Jim would walk back toward the seats, tearing the tickets up that he had picked up off the floor and throwing them into the air. Now he and Lenny had just made five hundred each. If on the other hand, the horse would happen to win, which almost never happened, he would simply walk back and say that he didn't get to the window in time to make the bets. As crude and simple as it sounds, it always worked.

Lenny Basil looked like Ricardo Montabalm, had a charming accent, and dressed like someone out of *GQ*. He was personable and pleasant, and it was easy to see how he would woo the ladies. On the other hand, there was Vince D'Agostine, who also thought of himself a gigolo. As much as Lenny looked like Ricardo Montabalm, Vince D'Agostine was a cross between Quasimoto and Weird Al Yankovic. Myself, I'm nothing to brag about, but I have to tell you—Vince came up with some women that could use a little work. For instance, Angie was about five-foot-five high and about five-foot-five wide, she had face and neck hair with some sprinklings of warts, and she gave off the enchanting scent of expensive perfume mixed with a generous amount of sweat. Vince had outdone himself. But the show must go on.

This time they earned their pay. They were at the track again. Vince said that he was tired and asked if Jim would hug and kiss Angie. Jim looked him in the eye and told Vince that if he asked again, he would shoot him. No matter how much they took her for, she got her money's worth. Jim kept her laughing, and Vince romanced her. She had a great sense of humor and friendliness, and even the rogues enjoyed themselves. Jim got an attack of conscience and fixed Angie up with little Nicky, who was Angie's male counterpart and a head shorter than her. Angie and Nicky became soul mates, and you couldn't separate them with a spatula. It was a marriage made in heaven. Nicky had never made a good living, but Jim always took care of him. Now Jim made him financially independent. Nick needed Angie; Angie needed Nick. Don't get misty-eyed yet. Jim had a move in store for Nick: they would become partners as bookies. They each put up a hundred thousand. Now they had a bank of two hundred thousand.

In this particular scheme, Jim would have one of his cohorts bet with them as a legitimate customer. He would pretend to be a high roller and bet between ten and twenty thousand at a shot. Then Jim would get the race results off the wire circuits, and unbeknownst to Nick, some races would go off several minutes ahead of schedule. So Jim's shill would call Nick and place a bet already knowing the winner, but with Nick thinking the race had not started yet. At the same time legitimate calls would be coming in from betters, so Nicky never knew what hit him. With only the information from the racing form that gave the post time, Nick never realized that he was being past-posted. The big bets only came when Nick was answering the phones, and it wasn't long before they went broke. To take the suspicion off himself, Jim put up another thirty thousand to keep them in business and said that their luck had to change. However, in a short time, they lost that too. Nick volunteered to pay half of the extra thirty that Jim put back up. Jim said this was not necessary, but if Nick really wanted to, he could give back the money whenever he got it, and Nick told him not to worry about it.

Now Jim had cleared $115,000 on this scam because only Nicky's money was lost. Jim justified his actions, knowing that Nicky was a degenerate gambler and would eventually lose it at the track anyway. Jim figured it was like a finder's fee for finding Nick a rich girlfriend. Nick and Angie got married or at least lived together. Nick loved gambling so much that eventually Angie told Nick to get a job to feed his habit. So then Nick began working for me as a clerk in an adult bookstore that I own but that's another story.

Jim Charms the Cops

One spring my old man and I were going to the track down in Maryland (we lived in Philadelphia) to see Gay Star, another one of Jim's horses, run. Jim was speeding, weaving in and out of traffic, trying to get to the track in time to bet his horse. I was on the floor of the car praying when a state trooper stopped us. I thought, "There is a God."

The officer said to Jim, "I've been trying to catch you for five miles."

Jim responded, "If I'd known that, you never would have caught me."

I was thinking, "Now we're going to jail."

Instead, the cop said, "Does that car have a Thunderbird engine in it?" It was a 1956 Ford station wagon with a Thunderbird engine in it.

Jim, who drove fast and hard all of the time and all over the place, responded, "I took the fuckin' thunder out of it; there's just the bird left." The officer laughed and Jim told him he was in a hurry to get to the track to bet on his horse. He said it was going to win.

The cop said, "Are you sure he's gonna win?"

The old man said, "I'll bet my balls on it." He told the cop the horse's name and what race he was in.

The cop said, "Follow me. I'll get you there on time." The cop gave us an escort to the track with flashing lights, the whole nine yards. We got to the track with time to spare. The cop gave my father fifty dollars to bet and said to my father, "If this friggin' horse doesn't win, don't even think about coming back to Maryland!" The track was either Laurel or Bowie; I can't remember which. The cop told my father that he would be at a diner when he was off-duty and gave him directions. Jim said he would be there after the races with his winnings. Gay Star won, and Jim headed for the diner, which was on our way home anyway (what luck the old man had).

When we pulled up to the diner, it was full of cops. They had all gotten a tip from their buddy and had bet on the horse, most likely with a bookie. I don't even want to think what would have happened if the horse had lost. We would have had all those angry cops on our ass, and we never would have made the border. In situations like this, Jim had a stock answer: "Frig 'em." Nothing ever bothered him. Jim went into the diner, bought dinner, and entertained everyone, having a good time laughing and carrying on. The cops gave him several numbers and asked him to let them know when his horses were running again; they said they would meet him at the Maryland-Delaware state line and escort him to the track. When we left the diner, they did everything but blow us kisses. In the future Jim met up with those guys and gave them winners most of the time. Jim was always diversified in his business dealings with the law and the unlawful. By the way, Jim never did get a ticket for speeding.

Jim's Inspection Station

Jim had a brush with the law. He had four thousand auto inspection stickers. He lived in Philadelphia, PA and under Pennsylvania Motor Vehicles Code all vehicles registered in the state must undergo an annual inspection by a licensed mechanic at an authorized inspection station. For some people this could be quite expensive running in the hundreds of dollars in repairs, where a hot sticker would cost about twenty bucks. He was in front of his house scraping an old sticker off his windshield and putting a hot one on when a cop car pulled up. The cops, looking at him and shaking their heads, asked, "Jim, what are you doing?"

Without hesitation he replied, "What's it look like, you assholes? I'm inspecting my car!" With that, the cops laughed, waved at him, and drove away. I guess Jim had an in with those guys. It was strange how it seemed that even the cops were on his side. I guess he just took care of everybody.

The Sure Thing

As I got older, I wanted to bet on a sure thing like Jim did. I wanted to make some money and get in on the action. I was working full-time at a can company, barely cranking out a living. I was a newlywed with a lot of bills, and I could use a break. I thought that betting on one of Jim's scams was the way to go. So I told him to let me know the next time he had a horse running, and he did. The horse's name was Chattanooga, and he was running at Garden State Race Track in New Jersey.

On race day, Jim, my uncle Barney, my uncle Frank (who wasn't really my uncle; he was actually my fathers cousin), another guy I didn't know (who I think had something to do with giving the horse the stuff), and I were all ready and eager. The horses came out on to the track. I noticed that Chattanooga had a red band around his girth (belly), and it had a pocket for the horse's genitals; in other words, he was wearing a jockstrap. I asked Jim, "Why is the horse wearing a jockstrap?" He said that that was one of the reasons the horse was a long shot: he had sore balls. I asked what the other reasons were. My father said that the horse also had bad legs and trouble breathing, and he had never won before. He said not to worry because the horse's legs were iced, and if they stayed numb, he'd have no trouble. They smoked his head to clear his sinuses. Smoking is something they do to make his nose run and clear his head. If his jockstrap didn't break, and his sore balls didn't bounce around and hit his legs, everything would go smoothly. I was afraid to ask if the horse was blind. He didn't seem to be in the best of shape. Knowing this, I went right ahead because I was one of the boys. I didn't have a lot of money, and I had borrowed what I did have, five hundred dollars, from the Oxford Loan Company in Philadelphia. The payback was for three years at $32.09 per month. This was a lot for me to bite off, but I had a sure thing, and I was now one of the boys.

Personally, I admit that I was shitting myself because I thought that was all the money in the world. Before I knew it, the bet was made: two hundred to win, two hundred to place, and a hundred to show (this means first, second, and third). The horse went off with odds at over fifty to one. It had been ninety-nine to one, but I guess our bets dropped the odds to fifty. We were probably the only brain surgeons that bet on him. The horses were at the gate. I was not ready for what happened next. They started right in front of the grandstands, and I had a clear view. Then they were off, and my heart was beating so fast and hard that I could feel it in my head. My eyes were fixed on that red jockstrap. Chattanooga broke in front and was pulling away from the pack. Uncle Barney was going nuts, yelling and screaming and kissing everybody. As the horses went around the clubhouse turn, Chattanooga was in front. I was yelling with everyone else. Down the backstretch they flew, and Chattanooga was out in front by five lengths and was "going away." Now everyone was congratulating each other and I truly was one of the boys. Around the far turn they came, Chattanooga leading the way by ten lengths. It was money in the bank. The horse went off at fifty-one odds and I was going to be rich. But at the top of the homestretch, it happened, like a nightmare. Chattanooga slowed up a little and began running with his back legs far apart. Jim said his balls hurt. Then his head started to bob up and down. He was breathing like an asthma patient. Jim said, "It don't look good, and he's got a way to go." The other horses were catching him fast. And then his legs thawed out, and he stopped short of the finish line. I felt sorry for the poor horse as he limped across the finish. He was walking like a duck, trying not to hurt his balls. I lost everything.

If anyone looked and felt worse than old Chattanooga, it was me. I could ill afford to pay a loan for two years. It was $32.09 for twenty-four months. "What am I going to tell my wife?" I said to Jim. I had lost five hundred dollars, and back then, that was a lot of money.

He said, "Son, let that be a lesson to you: you shouldn't gamble."

I replied, "I thought it was a sure thing."

Jim said, "Son, the only sure thing in life is there is no sure thing."

The other guys just shrugged it off and began looking at their racing programs to get ready to bet the next race. I took it in a different way. I was constipated for three days, I ran a fever, and I had to work overtime at the factory to pay the loan off early. But down the road, I would stick my nose in again.

Father Grab-a-Buck

I wasn't the only newcomer who wanted in on the action. Our parish priest, Father Lyons, came to our house around 1954 to collect money for something called block collection for St. Joan of Arks Church and School when Jim happened to be home. The priest knocked on our door, and Jim answered it. My mother was in the kitchen and said, "Who is it, Jim?"

Jim looked at the priest and turned to my mother and said, "It's Father Grab-a-Buck." My mother always prayed to Saint Rita, and this occasion was no exception. As she prayed out of one side of her mouth, out the other side of her mouth she told Jim he was going to burn in hell and she was going to send him there. Jim said, "If I'm gonna burn in hell, then I don't have to give this bandit any money." Jim turned and said to the priest, "You got a good racket—put your collar on backwards, throw a little water around, and get five hundred. Could you use a partner?"

By now my mother was on her knees, begging for forgiveness and telling Jim that lightning was going to strike him on his head. The priest laughingly smiled and said, "I'm Father Lyons, one of your parish priests."

Jim extended his hand, and as they shook hands, Jim said, "I'm Jimmy D'Angelo, one of your parish victims. Come on in and join the fun." My sister and I were holding my mother back to calm her down; she was still yelling at Jim that she was going to send him to hell early. As she so eloquently put it, she was going to kick Jim's pagan dago ass back to Italy. The priest could barely keep from laughing. The priest stayed cool, and Jim liked that. Jim said, "When you're done fleecing my old lady, if you want to join some real pirates, you can come to the track with me and my crew."

To everyone's surprise, Father Lyons said, "I'd love to." This was the beginning of a beautiful friendship.

The people in the neighborhood were betting whether the priest would convert Jim or Jim would convert the priest. The smart money was on Jimmy D. Jim said to the priest, "I'm half-Catholic. I don't pray, but I do go to bingo." Yes Jim had a bingo hustle. He would find a worthy charity, such as the Jewish war vets, the American Legion, or any credible nonprofit organization looking to raise money. He'd use their hall, and he would supply everything else, giving them a guarantee against the percentage. He would guarantee them ten thousand dollars or 50 percent, whichever was larger; if they only made twelve thousand dollars, the charity got its ten and Jim's boys got two. If they made thirty thousand, which was usually the case, the charity then got 50 percent, which would be fifteen thousand, and Jim and his entourage got the other fifteen thousand. They wanted to do business with Jim because the guarantee was more than they could make on their own. Jim would advertise a very large bingo jackpot; whereas the jackpot had previously been one thousand dollars or fifteen hundred, it was now ten thousand, and all the other games during the evening were doubled. This brought the players out of the woodwork and took the game from a half-filled hall to a sellout. It didn't matter how big the jackpot was; no one was going to win it. The crowd would win the small pots, twenty or fifty bucks, but the hundred- or five-hundred-dollar bonus games, along with the big jackpot, were won by the shills. But the hype of all the money that supposedly *could* be won filled the hall to overflowing. They actually had to turn people away with double, sometimes triple, the attendance, and with several bonus games, it was easy for Jim to make his guarantee and a bundle for him and his boys. On bingo night, Jim's crew supplied all the help, from the number caller to the card sellers. When it came time for the bonus games or the jackpot, they sold special cards for each of those games. Jim would have shills playing in the crowd, and the shills would be given winning cards. It didn't matter what numbers came out of the tumbler; the guy would call the numbers that were on the shills' cards. For example, if B10 came out of the tumbler' and the shills needed B4, the caller would just simply say B4 and so on until the caller had called all the numbers that the shills needed to win. When the shill won, he would holler "bingo," and one of the shills working the floor would come down and call out the relevant numbers that were on the shills' card, and the number caller would verify the bingo. No one was checking the number caller, and he simply threw the balls back into the tumbler for the next game. Now I'm not saying that Jim and Father Lyons worked together, but one year after they met, the nuns moved into a brand spanking new convent. The Lord moves in mysterious ways.

Jim's Savings and Loan

In that same neighborhood, Jim loaned money so that people could go into business, running restaurants, dry cleaners, used-car dealerships, and the like. Jim did not just loan money; he ensured success. If it was a restaurant, he would get all the restaurant equipment at low fell-off-the-truck prices, not to mention his meat and produce connections. One place that comes to mind was the Avenue Restaurant. It was owned by a colorful character named Whitey Chechi. Whitey had three sons, John, Mickey, and Edwin. Edwin's nickname was Bluef. Bluef stood about five-foot-ten, was close to four hundred pounds, and was a gentle soul, but Whitey, Mickey, and John were wild men. John played professional baseball, but I'm not sure what team. I think it was either the Phillies or the St. Louis Cardinals farm team as a catcher. Mickey, Bluef, and Whitey worked for a trucking company. Mickey and Whitey drove, and Bluef was a dispatcher. With that whole family working for the trucking company, you guessed it—Jim went into the trucking business.

Whitey's wife Kitty was also very heavy. She was five-foot-two and two hundred pounds, and like my mother, who didn't take any shit from Jim, Kitty didn't take any shit from Whitey. Kitty worked and ran the restaurant, and she hired young girls to do the footwork—the waitressing and busing tables and so on. She helped out in the kitchen and sometimes out on the floor when things got busy. The restaurant was located across the street from St. Joan of Ark's Church and School. On bingo night the place was mobbed with hungry losers. The school had a dance on Saturday night that filled the place with youthful sinners. On Sunday, mass (church services) filled the restaurant with the breakfast crowd of sinners and losers. Whitey and Kitty had a good location and a thriving business, praise the Lord and Jimmy D'Angelo.

When our family would go there to eat, Kitty would hug and kiss the whole bunch of us. Come to think of it, she was always hugging and kissing someone. Her pleasant personality definitely did not hurt business. Kitty's main job in the restaurant was keeping Whitey out of the cash register. He would steal money to go to the track with Jim. Whitey had two weaknesses: going to the track and losing his money and playing cards with Jim. We know how that turned out.

Whitey was about sixty years old but had the body of a much younger man. He was muscled and cut. He stayed in shape long before it was popular. Whitey, Jim, my uncle Tom Cucci, and Ed Wyke were at Garden State Race Track. My uncle Tom owned a place in south Jersey called Tom's Garden World, a very successful business he ran with his three sons and his wife. Ed Wyke had a real estate office two or three doors away from Whitey's restaurant. On this day they were leaving the track, Whitey had lost all of his money. Whitey said, "I'll bet you a hundred dollars that I can do a handstand down the escalator, from the top floor down to the main floor."

The boys shouted back, "You're on!" That old sucker went up on his hands, and down the escalator he went. The boys figured they couldn't lose. If he killed himself, or if he made it, it was worth a hundred bucks. They made noises, and they whistled and stamped their feet, trying to break his concentration, but through it all Whitey made it all the way down to the bottom. His face as red as a beet and huffing and puffing, he jumped up on his feet while still gasping for air and said, "Pay up, you assholes. Dinner's on me." That was in the 1950s, when a hundred bucks still bought dinner. Jim was laughing so hard that they thought they would have to give him oxygen. If anything seemed to be missing with Jim and his friends, it was fear. They had no fear of life. They all had a good time, and Jim brought this out in them.

PART II

The Puddle Jumper

On another day, when going to watch one of Jim's horses run, my mother, Uncle Barney, Uncle Frank, Uncle Tom, Dave Ginsberg (Jim's horse trainer), and I were walking toward the stable area when Jim spotted a huge puddle caused by a recent rain. The puddle stretched from the side of the road to the front of the stable. Jim said for a hundred bucks he could keep his feet together and, without a running start, could jump over the puddle. My uncle Tom was the first to say, "Jim, you'll never get your fat ass airborne." The others agreed, and the bet was on.

Jim squatted down, throwing his arms forward and backward to get momentum, and then he leaped. To everyone's amazement he cleared the puddle, but his momentum carried him head first into a stable post where they tie up horses, sending him ass-over-head backward into the muddy water. There wasn't a dry eye in the house.

With Jim lying flat on his back, my mother commented, "You look like a beached whale in a thousand-dollar suit." Everyone else was laughing so hard that they couldn't talk.

Jim, still on his back, argued, "I cleared the puddle," but he got no sympathy from that crowd.

Uncle Tom said, "We didn't see it; you'll have to do it again."

Jim, wiping himself off, smiled and said, "Tom, don't make me shoot ya."

My mother couldn't wait to get home to tell anyone who would listen. My mother loved to break Jim's balls, and Jim liked it; he had sporting blood.

Furniture Magic

When Jim was playing, he had fun. When he was stealing, he had fun. When he went to work at his furniture business, he made that fun. One time, he had a job to fix a cigarette burn on a dining room tabletop. Jim could do an invisible patch job in the home without having to take the entire table out to be refinished. He considered himself the best. And it may sound biased coming from me, but he was the best. This process took him about twenty or forty minutes, depending on the finish he had to match and the size of the damage. What he would do is take a very sharp knife and cut the burn out, leaving a notch or a shallow hole. Then he took something called a lacquer stick and, using a hot knife, melted it into the hole, and the melted lacquer filled the hole, after which Jim passed over it gently with a hot knife, smoothing the lacquer evenly. Next, with a very light sandpaper, he would sand it flush, leaving a light spot. Now Jim would go to work matching colors, staining over the spot and painting the grains back into the wood with a very fine sable brush. Finishing up with a little color and liquid lacquer on a pad—usually a rolled-up baby's diaper (they're good because they don't leave lint)—he would rub the pad on the spot, blending away the damage. Finally he would rub the whole tabletop, giving it a new hand-rubbed finish. I made this sound easier than it actually is. The damage would disappear, and this technique took years to perfect.

On this particular day, the damage was at the far end of a dining room table, and I was with my father on this job. Jim had finished and done a beautiful job. He called the woman into the room to look at it. She said, "I can still see it, and I wish it was better." She was full of crap, and the repair was invisible, but Jim smiled and told her to give him ten more minutes to work on it. She left the room.

I asked, "How are you going to make it better? It's invisible."

Jim said, "Grab an end of the table." We lifted it and turned it. Now the table's position was reversed, and what had been the right side of the table was now the left. The damage was at the opposite end of the table.

Jim waited ten minutes and called the woman back into the room. She looked at where she thought the damage was and said, "You're very good, but I can still see it." She was looking at the undamaged end of the table.

Jim said, "Would you mind kneeling with us?" She asked why. Jim answered, "We're going to pray because only the Lord could please you." She gasped, and Jim showed her what he had done. Her face dropped and turned red. Jim said, "Now get it up!" and he got paid. When we got into the car, he looked at me and said, "If they ever make murder legal, she's the first to go." He smiled, and we drove away.

In a similar story, Jim was sent by John Wanamaker's department store to a customer's home to inspect a chair. The chair that he was to inspect was three years old. The client's complaint was that no one ever used it yet it was falling apart. When Jim and I got to the house, the lady let us in and walked us into the living room. She pointed to a chair that sat in front of the TV. Jim said, "What's the problem?"

The lady said, "Look at it. It's falling apart and no one uses it." She wanted John Wanamaker's to reupholster it or replace it at no cost to her. She said it was defective. Jim looked at it and saw that the material was worn thin. He turned it upside down, and the bottom was sagging. She repeated, "No one ever sits in it." To me it looked more like someone had slept in it.

After giving it a thorough going-over, Jim said, "There is only one way this will never happen again."

She said, "How's that?"

Jim answered, "You're gonna have to hire a detective because when you're not looking, someone is sitting in your chair." She threw both of us out. Jim was laughing and said, "The old broad's got balls." He turned in a recommendation that the store replace the chair free of charge.

I Can't Steal It Fast Enough

One afternoon, Jim was at his kitchen table complaining about money. He was saying that no matter how much money he made, it was never enough. "This family spends it faster than I can steal it, and that's pretty fucking fast." He said, "Everyone's got a cross to bear, but why is mine made of platinum?"

I opened my big mouth and said, "Dad, what do you do with all your money?" He took a deep drag off of his cigarette, blew out the smoke, smiled, and winked while shaking his head knowingly, but he never answered me.

Fifteen years later, I had a family and a retail furniture store and all the problems and responsibility that go with it. We were sitting at my kitchen table this time when somehow the cost of living came up in the conversation. Up until this point, for the most part Jim had just been listening to everyone. I was pissing and moaning about the cost of doing business and the costs of a car, a house, a kid, and taxes and so on. And once again, Jim took a deep drag off of his cigarette, blew out the smoke, smiled, winked, and shook his head knowingly and said, "Son, what do you do with all your money?" He waited fifteen years, but he got me!

Another time in Jim's kitchen, my mother had a case of the "I wants." She was going down the list of the things that she wanted. She had been talking for about thirty minutes when Jim could take it no longer and jumped into the conversation and said, "Mary, I'm gonna find out what the fuck you don't want and buy a truckload of it." Well, you know about my mother and her temper. My brothers and I had to hold her while Jim escaped out of the house, allowing Mom to cool down.

Hustling Pool

Among Jim's other talents, he was also a pool hustler. No one knew how good he could play. When he was priming a victim, he would lose by just a little. As they raised the stakes, Jim would win by just a little, telling the mark that he was not playing any better but that he was just getting lucky, and the mark was a better player and was just choking (not doing his best).

One story that comes to mind is the time Jim played a guy who owned his own poolroom. They started by playing a game called Points. The object was to sink a hundred balls, and the first one to do so won the game. After convincing the owner, Joe Carangi, that Joe was the better player, Jim had to sink only eighty balls to win whereas Joe still had to sink a hundred. They started out waging five hundred a copy.(per game) Jim would win by getting to eighty just before Joe would get to a hundred, keeping the games close. Sometimes Joe would get too close and win, in about one game out of six.

They continued with Joe having to get to only eighty to win and Jim having to get to a hundred for a year because Jim kept Joe convinced that Joe was still the better player and that when he played Jim, he choked, and Joe agreed. Jim had Joe's mind and Joe's money, and eventually he won the poolroom too. Jim, testing his entrepreneurial ability, loaned Joe the money to buy back a half-interest in his own poolroom. Actually, the money he loaned Joe was the money he had won from him. Now Joe and Jim were partners.

Word got out that Jim owned half-interest in a poolroom, and business took off. There were wall-to-wall burglars, thieves, hustlers, and all types of underworld figures. They ran amateur tournaments and had lady's night and family night, and there was a private room called the VIP room where hustlers would take their clients and play for huge amounts of money; Jim and his new partner got a percentage. There were hot items for sale and after-hour card games, and an occasional hooker would pick up a high roller. Players of all levels came to hustle pool there.

Joe made enough money to buy back the poolroom, now named Moulin Rouge (pretty sexy). Jim still hung around, loan sharking and so on, and that was OK with Joe. Joe was making more money now than he ever had. Where there was Jim, there was business. Jim took a mediocre business and made it a hot spot. People would come there just to rub shoulders with the underworld figures. Jim talked to everyone who came in the place. He'd greet them at the door, and he knew them all by name; everyone felt special. For years this remained Jim's office. Don't get misty-eyed over Jim giving Joe another chance to own his own poolroom and Joe making more money than he ever did. Where there's money, there's Jim.

Equal Opportunity Lender

Jim also loaned money for the mob. The guy he put the money on the street for was from south Philadelphia, and Jim put the money on the street uptown in northeast Philadelphia. The mob guy's name was Frankie Sindone. He had a restaurant on Passyunk Avenue called Frank's Cabana Steaks. The food was great, and the atmosphere was even better. It was just like in the movies—five or six guys sitting around at a table in the back playing cards and a couple of bodyguards sitting at the counter. Frank was in the back room doing business.

I was nine years old the first time there. I'd go in and sit at the counter and eat whatever I wanted for free. I thought that was a big deal. The mob guys would tease me and ask me, "Hey kid, are you getting any?"

And I'd answer, "Getting any what?"

And they'd say, "If you don't know, then you ain't getting any," and they'd laugh.

I'd shrug it off. I wasn't there for the conversation; I was there for a free cheesesteak. As you might of heard those babies are good. However, the money wasn't made in the restaurant; it was made in loan-sharking, numbers, and bookmaking. Being the iron-balled enterprising man that he was, Jim put not only the mob's money on the street but his own as well. People knew he was loaning money to the boys so that they would make their payments. Jim figured this was a no-risk situation, so half the money he loaned was the mob's, and the other half of the money he loaned was his. The mob had a partner and never knew it. If he had gotten caught, this book would be half as long.

Sometimes I thought he had a computer chip for a brain. Everything that he did he kept in his head. He took numerous bets on horses and loaned money to several people for various amounts, but even though he never wrote anything down, he knew where every nickel was and who got what and who didn't. One day he asked me to go for a ride with him to collect a vig (that's short for vigerage, which means interest) on a loan. If someone couldn't make their regular payment, then they would just pay their interest.

We went to New Jersey to an adult bookstore. Even though I was thirty-six years old at the time, I had never been inside an adult bookstore. There were booths you could go into, and when you closed the door behind you, there was total darkness with the exception of the light from a bill acceptor that took ones, fives, tens, and twenties. For one dollar, a shade would go up, revealing a piece of glass. Behind the glass a light would go on, and on the other side would be a small booth with a scantily clad woman. There were phones on both sides. You could pick up the phone, and she would do the same. You could talk to her for about forty seconds before the friggin' shade would come down. Then it would cost another buck.

This fellow had twelve of these booths plus thirty-five peep show booths, which worked the same way, but you only got to view an X-rated movie. These booths cost thirty-five cents, and you got about a minute of viewing time. The timers in all the booths allowed you to put in as much money as you wanted. Some guys spent hours in them. About now you're doing the math. It was a real moneymaker. In the front of the store, there were books, videos, sexual aids, lotions, and potions for sale. This guy was raking it in. You name it; he had it. It looked like a human spare parts department. This was a pretty sexy place.

The owner was a degenerate gambler, so Jim had a customer for life. Jim said that he always owed at least ten thousand, and the interest was two thousand, and he never paid more than the interest, so he was a pretty good customer. As nuts as it seems, the guy couldn't wait to see Jim from week to week. He was happy when Jim would show up, and he was sad to see him go. I think he enjoyed owing the mob—it gave him a sense of adventure—and when he was late with the payment, Jim was stern with him. I think that made his day. Although a tongue-lashing was all he got from Jim, I think he would have liked a spanking. It takes all kinds.

At this time, I owned a furniture store in Huntington Valley. The store was near the Huntington Valley–South Hampton border—hence Hampton Valley Furniture Store. I was working seven days a week, and this guy with the bookstore made more in one month than I made in a year. Three months to the day after I learned this, Hampton Valley Furniture was history, and Fantasy Island was born—and that's another book!

Blaze Star

Over the years, living with my father, we moved seven times. No matter what location, the old man made friends immediately. People were always in and out of our house. Between my mother's friends, my father's cronies, my sister and brothers' friends, and my friends, we never knew who was at the house.

One day, I walked into the kitchen at the house on Evans Street in Philadelphia, and a stripper very well-known at that time by the name of Blaze Star was sitting at the table, having tea with my mother. I was about fourteen. I'm telling you, I couldn't have been happier as I stood there grinning. My dad introduced me and then told me to beat it. Believe me: the thought crossed my mind.

Blaze was visiting my uncle Barney and his wife Patty. Patty was also in show business; she was a singer and pretty good at it. After Barney and Patty introduced Blaze to Jim, the two became friends, and my father purchased a horse from the brother of Blaze's boyfriend; the brother had a horse ranch (perhaps in Maryland). Blaze's boyfriend at the time was much older and also a governor. The horse my father purchased from the governor's brother was going to be named Blaze Star, but at the time, the governor was trying to keep a low profile about his relationship with Blaze, so Jim named the horse Gay Star. Gay Star, like his indirect namesake, made a name for himself and made some money too.

Meeting celebrities and public figures was commonplace for my uncle Barney and for my uncle Sal, too, whose stage name was Lenny Patton. It was hard to tell who was the celebrity because everyone would hover around Jim like bees to honey. Jim was a natural-born entertainer. Women would always try to hug and kiss him, but he would pull away and say, "If you want to get me all excited, cut the shit and give me a pound of fifties." The more he resisted, the more they teased. One aunt in particular, my aunt Jeanie, Lenny Patton's wife, took particular joy in teasing him. He was such a tough guy, and in any situation he could stand his ground, but my Aunt Jeanie could make him blush.

Mickey Mouse Club

I came home from school one day, and four guys with dark suits and shoulder holsters were all leaning forward in their chairs, engrossed in the TV. They were watching the *Mickey Mouse Club*. This was a sight. Someone of mob importance was meeting with Jim in the kitchen. I walked in the room and passed between the Mouseketeers and the musketeers, blocking the men's view of the TV, and one of them politely but firmly said, "Hey kid, sit your ass down." I did.

Selling the Mausoleum

I told you that we moved seven times. One of the moves didn't last long. We moved into a development where only 10 percent of the homes were completed and the other 90 percent were not quite finished. There were three different styles, and they repeated over and over. Why Jim was there, we'll never know. There was style A, then style B, then style C, then style A, then style B, then style C, and so on and so on. To make matters worse, there weren't any street signs or streetlights. After being there about three days, Jim came home one night and couldn't find his house. The place was full of cul-de-sacs and dead ends. He was pissed! He got the cops to bring him home and then brought them in for coffee and cake. Everyone was laughing at Jim, and he loved it. He turned to my mother and said, "I'm selling this fuckin' mausoleum!" And in two weeks we were gone.

Mary, I Need the Soap

Jim had no problem getting laughs. One morning, my mother was having coffee with my aunts Jean, Clara, Lil, Frances, and Liz. Jean was my uncle Lenny Patton's wife, and Liz was the wife of my uncle Mike (my mother's brother). Clara and Lil were sisters and had been very close friends with my mom and dad since childhood; they were not blood, but I always knew them as aunts, and the same went for my Aunt Francis. All these ladies were tots together and inseparable and loved Mary and Jim very much. As far as they were concerned, Jim and Mary could do no wrong. There are many stories about the fun-filled times they had together in the past. I can't explain how close this group was.

Getting to the story at hand, this morning, the girls were in the kitchen having coffee and cake. Jim was in the shower. He didn't have any soap, so he opened the bathroom door a crack and yelled, "Mary, I need soap!" There was soap under the kitchen sink in the cabinet. My mother was in the middle of a story and was going to finish it before getting the soap and giving it to Jim, but Jim was impatient and yelled again even louder; that did not sit well with mom. Then came the third yell: "Mary, I need the friggin soap!"

With this Mary said to the girls, "Well, he'll just have to friggin' wait," and went on with her story.

Then Jim whistled very loud and yelled, "Mary, where's the friggin soap??"

This pushed Mom over the edge. She said to the group, "Who does he think he's calling? His dog?" and went on talking. Then there was a silence for the next ten minutes. You could hear the shower running, but no more yelling and no more whistling. Then Jim appeared in the kitchen, all five-foot-ten, two hundred and thirty pounds of him, dripping wet and naked as the day he was born.

With no expression he calmly and slowly walked over to the cabinet where the soap was stored under the sink, squatted down with his ass to the ladies, reached under the cabinet in plumber fashion, and retrieved the soap. Slowly standing and turning full front to the group, holding the soap between his thumb and his forefinger, he said softly, "Never mind, Mary, I got it myself," and then he slowly turned and walked out of the room.

The girls were choking on their coffee and cake, spitting it all over each other and laughing so hard that I thought we'd need the rescue squad. They actually fell out of their chairs. It took some time for them to get their composure. One would start again, and then the whole group would start laughing their heads off. My mom, much to my surprise, was laughing as hard as the rest of them. In all, it must have gone on for half an hour. After that, whenever they would get together, someone would bring it up, and they would get hysterical all over again. My mother never got angry with Jim; she just laughed.

I Ain't Dead

Around the same time as the soap incident, a friend of Jim's passed away. His name was Jimmy Dodd. My mother always got very emotional when anything like this happened. She'd send flowers and mass cards, say the rosary, make novenas, and light candles, and so on. To say that Jim, on the other hand, took things in stride is an understatement.

The morning of the funeral, Jim was going out the door, and Mom said, "They're burying Jimmy Dodd today."

Jim answered, "That's because he's dead."

Mom said, "Where the hell do you think you're going?"

Jim answered, "To the racetrack."

"Why?" asked Mom.

"Because I ain't dead," he replied, and out the door he went.

Carrying the Leg

As colorful as Jim was, his friends and relatives ran a close second. Take my Uncle Frank for instance. Every other word out of his mouth was a curse word. He talked about five decibels above a shout. When he thought he was right, he would argue with Jesus. Uncle Frank stood about six feet tall, and he was portly with a round red face. He'd been known to drink a little wine, but he claimed it was for medicinal purposes. He had his right leg cut off close to the hip and his left leg badly scarred from a train accident. He had worked for the railroad and had somehow fallen under the cars. I don't know all the particulars of how it happened. Sometimes he would be in great pain. When this happened, he was less than pleasant. Actually, he was a fourteen-carat pain in the ass. If he didn't take his medicine, he would drink a little booze. So when we traveled with Frank, my old man made sure there was a bottle of something close by. This sweetened his disposition and provided entertainment for the boys watching a half-hit-in-the-ass, one-legged guy on crutches.

He wore a prosthetic leg, but after a few hours his stump would hurt, and he would take it off, no matter where he was, in private or in public. He would drop his pants, stand there in his shorts, and take off his leg. The first time I saw, this I was about eight. When I was there, he'd give it to me to take care of, and then he would walk on his crutches, and I would follow him dragging the leg. When I was older, about fourteen, his favorite place to take his leg off was the racetrack. Not much had changed. I would still follow him around, but now I was big enough to carry the leg and that beat dragging it. I hated it. When I would complain to my dad, he'd laugh and say, "Throw it the fuck way!"

Uncle Frank, hearing this, would say something like, "You insensitive prick. I'm a cripple. Show some respect and watch your foul mouth in front of the kid." When Frank took his leg off, it was quite unique-looking. I don't know what it was made of, but it felt like concrete. He had a black work boot with a thick rubber sole and a heavy-duty heel. The prosthetic had the same sock on it for the last eight years of his life (it was sort of an army brown, although it may have been white at some point). On his good leg he wore a boot that matched, and he did

51

change that sock once in a while. Whatever sock he wore on his good leg never matched the other leg.

At the track, Frank would leave his seat to go to the men's room and would leave his leg standing in his seat. He said it kept people out of his seat and made it easier to find when the place was crowded. What a lovely sight it was, protruding up from the seat. Guess who got to sit next to it. If you guessed me, you're right. I guess I was the low man on the totem pole. With my carrying the leg around and being in charge of it, the guys would tease me and hit me with corny jokes like, "Hey Bern, I didn't know you were a leg man." At the time I didn't think it was funny, but now I look back at it and laugh. Being teased by those guys meant acceptance. No one was above being teased, including my old man.

Uncle Frank got his too. One day after all the races were over and everybody was "tap city" (broke), we were leaving the track when someone said to Frank, who didn't have his leg on, "Give him a cup and maybe he can make enough money so we can go to the night races at Brandywine." Frank replied with fifteen minutes of profanity and comeback insults that had everyone rolling on the ground. Believe it or not, this was the way these guys kept their spirits up. Nothing was ever taken as an insult; it was just a game.

Barney the Entertainer

Frank's better half was the direct opposite of Frank; her name was Gert. She was quiet and never spoke much above a whisper. While Frank was out with the boys at the racetrack, she would hang out with my mother and other racetrack widows such as my Aunt Patty (married to my uncle Barney, my father's brother). Barney was the comedian. He had the energy level of a hummingbird on espresso. He would perform all day and all night and never got tired. He'd sing, dance, do impressions, and tell jokes nonstop.

When they would come home from the track to our house, my mother would have dinner cooking. Barney would walk in and sing and dance for my mother. He'd sing "Mammy" like Al Jolson and then start to rifle off one-liners while dancing and juggling anything he could get his hands on—fruit, knives, forks, and so on. One time, the boys had been listening to this all day. They told my father that they couldn't take any more, and if he didn't shut up, they would shoot him.

Jim replied, "It's not his fault; when he was a kid, he spent too much time in the bathroom playing with his pump gun." Then Barney crossed his eyes, stuck his tongue out the side of his mouth, and pretended to play with his pump gun. The man was simply insane. Jim said, "Barney, even a fuckin' train stops."

Then Barney would reach out to grab Jim, saying in a childlike voice, that he wanted to "kissy wissy" his "oochy poochy baby brother."

Jim said, "I'm gonna save you guys the trouble. I'm gonna kill him myself!" The only thing that could put a stop to the "grab assing" happened next: Mom announced that dinner was ready. The table was set for a small army. Typically there would be twelve to fourteen people. The mood was good, and so was Mom's cooking. While the women said grace, the boys dug in like vultures. These guys ate like piranhas. There was never anything left, and they'd have eaten the chairs if you'd let them. All the food would go and this made Mom happy.

Mom on the Attack

Like the characters in Jim's life, Mom had a few quirks of her own. I'll give you a little background. One day I took her to the supermarket. When we were done shopping, we got in the car. We left the lot and were almost home when a guy on a motorcycle ran a stop sign. I stopped just in time. Instead of the cyclist being thankful, he flipped us the bird. Normally, this wouldn't bother me, and it took more than a fleeting bird to bother my mother. But I had been training for an upcoming fight at the Spectrum in Philadelphia (at this time I was a pro welterweight), and I guess my patience was a little thin. I was to box the next day.

Well, I had a block to go to the house, so I dropped Mom off, went around the block, and caught the guy at a red light. He had a girl on the back. She had a six-pack of beer in one hand and was holding on with the other. I got out of my car and told the girl to get off the bike because I was going to kick the shit out of her boyfriend. She got off, and the guy got off and grabbed a can of beer, threatening to throw it at me if I came close. From behind me I heard a voice. It was Mom; she had taken a shortcut between the houses. She said, "Bernard, tear his friggin' heart out. Kick the living shit out of the gutless bastard!" Then Mom started on the girl, saying, "Are you with this gutless asshole? If you are, you should be ashamed. My son is half his size, and that big pussy you're with is going to throw beer cans." She said to me, "Don't fight with him, Bernard; he might hit you with a can, and if you get cut, you won't be able to fight tomorrow. I'll kick the shit out of this blowhard."

With that said, Mom went after the guy. I grabbed her, and she was yelling, "Let me go, I'll kill the gutless bastard." At this point the girl was petrified, and the blood had drained from the face of her boyfriend. Visibly shaken, they jumped on their bike and sped away. Mom broke loose and chased them halfway down the block like a barking dog chasing traffic. By the way, Mom was no spring chicken; she was fifty-two and still not taking any shit. She came back from her chase still pissed and said, "You shouldn't have held me, I would have kicked the shit out of the pair of them." I can only imagine what those two thought. Seeing me and Mimsy in action, especially Mimsy, they must have thought they were in the *Twilight Zone* or a scene from *The Texas Chainsaw Mas-*

sacre. When Mom gets pissed, she has all the charm of a pit bull on the attack. So you see that Jim's life was not all milk and honey because Mom got pissed at Jim from time to time, and he always did the smart thing—ran.

Mike and Liz

My mother's brother Mike—he was a hoot also, and he was married to a double hoot. Her name was Liz. My aunt Liz was also one of my mother's best friends. Liz was a wild one, and she liked to throw parties and have a good time. When it came to having fun, she was in with the right crowd. When my mother and Liz were teenagers, they went to a church dance with their friends just about every week on a Saturday night. One night, when the dance was over, Liz asked a guy they knew to give them a ride home. Being cute, the guy said, "What's in it for me?"

Liz, without batting an eye, replied, "Just a little dust from dancing." Liz could joke with the best of them. Later she would marry my mother's brother, Mike, who had a similar sense of humor. That marriage was made in heaven. By day, Mike worked for my dad refinishing furniture, and at night, my dad taught him how to be a hustler and a shill. He took to the nightlife like a fish to water. He loved the excitement and said it paid the mortgage. Jim corrupted everybody, and everybody loved it.

Bernie's Peter

My Aunt Clara, another right-hand man of my mother's (and she still is), was a liberated woman long, long before anyone had ever heard of women's lib. She loved men and made no bones about it. She also loved children; she raised foster children and a couple of her own. She was a very kind lady.

Like Mom, she didn't take any shit either. Back when we were living in Port Richmond, in Philly (I was about seven or eight at the time), I was sitting on my front stoop, looking down at a crowd of people. A man was beating up a woman. Working her way through the crowd was my Aunt Clara. She knew both of them. I don't remember the name of the woman who was getting hit, but the man's name was Jimmy Quick. His nickname was Quickie; I should have found out how he got that handle. Oh well, back to the story. Clara had made her way up to both of them and told Quickie to let her go and to stop the hitting. Quickie told her to mind her own fuckin' business or she'd be next; this was a mistake. Like a bolt of lightning, Clara threw a left and a right and knocked Quickie out for the night.

You see, Clara's dad trained amateur and professional fighters. Clara loved boxing and spent a lot of time in the gym. Now could you imagine my mother and Clara out shopping together and some unsuspecting mugger trying to mug them. You would almost feel sorry for the mugger. There wouldn't be much left of him when the "iron box twins" were done with him. My brother Jerry gave them that name, and oh boy, does it fit. The twins are ninety years old and haven't mellowed a bit. Clara still drinks, smokes, and chases men. My wife Gloria and I had a party when Clara was a bit younger, about eighty-two. Now after a night of drinking, smoking, dancing, and flirting with anyone in pants, it was time for her to go home, and I asked my very, very close friend, Peter Cordua, to take her to my brother Jerry's car. Clara was feeling no pain but was a little shaky, so Pete put his arm around her and held her tight. Clara, being true to her nature, with a flirtatious smile said, "Who are you?"

Pete replied, "Peter."

Clara said, "Oh, are you Bernie's Peter?"

Peter said, "Lady, I've been called a lot of things, but never Bernie's Peter," and then he gently put the old girl in the back of my brother's car.

Jim's Card Game

Jim ran a card game for local hoods out of his house on Evans Street in Philadelphia, and the game was on the up-and-up (there wasn't any cheating). Three quarters of the guys were hustlers and could spot anyone that was cheating. The remaining quarter were civilians looking for a thrill by rubbing elbows with the underworld: they were playing with the bad boys. The bad boys knew this and put on a little show from time to time by arguing, yelling, and cursing at each other. It was hard to tell if they were clowning or serious. This kept the civilians on edge.

Jim made money by running the game (usually some kind of poker, draw, or seven-card game or the like), keeping law and order, and providing food, booze, smokes, and a place to shower and sleep. These games ran for days, usually from a Friday to Monday, twenty-four hours a day nonstop. Jim made his money this way: every time the cards were dealt and the pot reached twenty-five dollars, he'd take a dollar. When it got to fifty, he'd take another dollar. When it got to a hundred, he'd take another dollar. So he would make between one and three dollars per hand dealt. This averaged out to a little better than a hundred dollars an hour, twenty-four hours a day for three days. He would take in six to eight thousand for the weekend.

He had four shills (and I was one) who would do four hours on (working the game being the house man). The house man sat at the table with the players. He kept the betting straight so that no one could say they threw money in the pot when they didn't, he expeditiously moved the game along so that the action did not slow up, he settled all arguments and disputes at the table, and most importantly, he took that dollar at the proper intervals. For this the shills were paid twenty-five dollars an hour, which back in the 1960s was good money.

The game ran from 1960 to 1965. The game ran three to six weeks, and then there would be a lull for about six to eight weeks before it would start up again. The underworld guys had colorful nicknames like Johnny Jumbo, Porky, The Chink, and Peter Rabbit (who, by the way, was a world-class pool hustler with names like Minnesota Fats on his victim list). Other card players there were Moon, The Whale, The Greek, Big Marvin, and Fast Eddie Derace (a bartender who lived in a penthouse, drove two new Cadillacs, had a large diamond pinky ring, and had thousands of dollars to gamble with—it makes you think he may have had a side job). Big Marvin's real name was Marvin Adleman, and he was a retired, professional, light heavyweight fighter who had fought Tiger Jones for the world championship. He was nobody to mess with.

One night, at about 4 AM, the phone rang. Before I could pick it up, Fast Eddie got it and said, "Hello baby, I told you never to call me here." Then he started a very sexy conversation, giving in graphic detail what he was going to do to her when he got home. Here's a sample of what he said: "I'm gonna stick it in every hole that you've got, and I know how you like it." I'll leave the rest to your imagination. Eddie was holding his hand over the phone, but he was talking loud enough for everyone to hear. He was pretending that we'd have to be eavesdropping to hear, but he knew exactly what he was doing. The game had ground to a halt; he had everyone's ear. There was suppressed giggling and laughing, and all of a sudden, Eddie handed the phone across the table and said, "Marvin, it's your wife." The players got hysterical, but Marvin on the other hand didn't and dove across the table at Eddie, grabbing at him but missing. Eddie ran up the stairs and yelled back at Marvin, "I'll see you at home!" This pissed Marvin off even more.

I held onto Marvin so that Eddie could make his escape while Marvin was screaming at him, "I'm gonna kill you, you creepy cock sucker!"

Jim, who was sleeping on a cot, woke up and said, "What the fuck's goin' on?" All the players volunteered to tell him. When he heard what Eddie had said on the phone and done to Marvin, he smiled, looked at Marvin, and said, "That's what you get for marrying the whore," and then went back to sleep.

We never knew who really was on the phone talking to Eddie, but it definitely was not Marvin's wife. It was someone for Eddie, and he had to leave, and this was just the way he planned the exit. Was Marvin really mad at Eddie? No. Was Eddie really running for his life? I don't think so. This was just another way to entertain the civilians and keep the game interesting, and there was always another player to fill the empty seat. And fill the empty seat they did. As soon as someone went bust, another victim took his place.

Even though there wasn't any cheating, these guys were top-notch players. They played smart, knowing when to hold and when to fold by reading the cards and each other's tells, any eye or body movement a player may exhibit when getting a good hand or trying to bluff a bad hand. For instance, when someone got a good hand, his voice might have gone lower or higher. These guys would pick that up. Or a player might fiddle with his cards, rush his bet, or be uncharacteristically calm. No matter how slight the mannerisms, these guys were sharp, and these movements would "tell" them whether they were bluffing or they had a good hand. It was definitely not a game for beginners; the game was by invitation, the table stakes were very high, and these players were well-heeled.

Despite all the money that was at the game, no one dared to rob it; with all the heavily armed arch criminals who were playing, robbers would never have gotten out alive. Outside of our house there was a telltale sign that something was going on inside; both sides of the streets were lined with new Cadillacs. Back then, Cadillacs were what the boys drove—except for Jim, who always low-keyed it. He drove a station wagon.

Fancy cars never excited him, but a good plan or a good scam would make him tingle all over. Other people tried to run their own games and lure Jim's players away, but Jim never lost his following. His strong personality and his relentless scheming kept their interest; they knew Jim was never without a thought or a plan to make money, and they wanted to be a part of it, and he knew how to pick through the crowd and who to cut in on his moneymaking schemes. It was like dangling a carrot in front of a rabbit, and if they hung out long enough they would make money with him. After all, half their Cadillacs were hot and retitled compliments of "Jim's auto sales." If you paid cash, you could buy a new car for about one-third the retail cost.

He also made money off the civilian players. If they went broke at the game, they would borrow money from you-know-who. Before there were ATMs, there was Jim. You didn't need a card or a pin number; you just asked (how easy is that?). Jim also loaned money to family—I should say "gave money," actually—and we had a big family. People were always borrowing for various reasons, and to the people he loved, he was a soft touch, which was just the opposite of what he had to be on the street. If anyone was having it tough, and he had it, that person got it (sometimes even when it was Jim's last buck). He was confident that he always could make more, and he did. My mother was a soft touch also, so if you didn't get it from Jim, you got it from Mary. This kept Jim wheeling and dealing, and he loved it. He would bitch and moan, but he never changed. He would just give, give, give; no one could figure him out. You couldn't get over on him, and you couldn't steal from him. He knew all the moves, but if he loved you, you just had to ask.

My First Cadillac

Considering that Jim had a sister, brothers, brothers-in-law, sisters-in-law, nieces, nephews, cousins, close friends, and charities that he gave to, it was no wonder he stole. Jim didn't consider cheating at gambling as stealing. He thought the money was better in his hands than with the casino. After all, who needed it more—him or Trump? He was saving people the trouble of going to Atlantic City or Vegas. He would come to your home and play cards. In his mind he made house calls; do casinos do that? He'd loan you back half of what you'd lost—try that at the Taj Mahal. Jim valued his friends. He never based a friendship on looks, money, or social standing. He based it on loyalty. He told me to think of the worst thing you could do, the worst trouble you could be in, and to then think of who would stand by you and not care if you're innocent or guilty. That's your friend. It works for me and keeps my feet on the ground.

I mentioned Dad getting Cadillacs. Well, he got me a beautiful 1954 Cadillac convertible, all black with dark red leather interior. I got it on a promise I would take my mother where she wanted to go—to see friends, to go food shopping, to go clothes shopping. My mother never got a driver's license, but she had a chauffeur-driven Caddy.

I first saw the car in a warehouse in the Kensington section of Philadelphia. It was between a bunch of cars parked inside a large closed-up building. You couldn't see the cars from the outside. I wondered how this guy Jerry, who owned the place, made a living when no one could see the cars from the street. Dad said he only took special orders. I was salivating to drive. I had just gotten my license, and the thought of a Caddy convertible had me in dreamland. I thought I might even get laid. It didn't matter how ugly you were; a Caddy convertible would do the trick. (However, in my case it wasn't enough, but don't cry for me; later, a Coupe de Ville did the trick!) Jerry said he couldn't have the convertible ready for delivery for two or three weeks. I didn't know it at the time, but he didn't have a title for it. He had a connection with junkyards, and when cars were total wrecks, they would sell him the titles, and somehow Jerry would put the title to a hot car (I know how, but I don't want to tempt anyone).

I waited two sleepless weeks, and finally, one day I came home from school, and there it was, a big, shiny, black lacquered beauty with sparkling chrome. I was in love. I couldn't wait to get my grubby little hands on it. I ran into the house, and my mom and dad both had shit-eating grins. They went over the list of duties that I was to do to earn the right to drive this extension of my manhood. It was big, it was black, and I was proud; black is beautiful! If they had asked me to thumbtack my eyelids open, I would have done it.

Then came the moment of truth. Dad asked me to pick up work orders at John Wanamaker's in Jenkintown, about ten miles away. He said, "Go alone and drive slow. If you get a ticket for speeding, I will break your legs and shove them up your ass, and you will never drive again!" Forget not being able to drive again; the thought of having my legs broken off and shoved up my ass got my attention. But being a sixteen-year-old and proud as a peacock of my new car, I picked up three friends. We drove over to Wanamaker's and picked up the work orders for Dad's furniture business. On the way back, I was going too fast to make a curve that was notorious for accidents. I realized I was going too fast and tried to brake, but there had been rain earlier, and the road was slick. I slid off and into a ditch at about twenty-five miles an hour. My front wheel hit a sewer pipe made of concrete, and this stopped the car almost immediately. Back then, there were no seatbelts, and if there had been, no one would have gotten hurt. Out of the four people in the car, one person in the backseat, who was sitting on her boyfriend's lap, got thrown forward and hit her head on the rearview mirror. The cops took the girl to the hospital to get three stitches up in her hairline, and the car had to be towed away. So then I was waiting for Jim to break my legs and, well, you know.

When Jim came into the hospital, his main concern was about who was hurt. He looked at me and said, "You hurt someone. Look at her. Now how do you feel?" I looked at the girl, whose name was Joan, and started to cry. He apologized to Joan's parents, and then it was my turn. These people were upset and dug into me; it was awful. I felt like I'd rather have my legs shoved up my ass. When I got home, I thought I was going to get it, but instead my father said, "Did you learn anything?" I had. The guilt and shame lasted longer than any beating. A beating would have left me off the hook. Jim knew me, and the way to get through was to let me punish myself. He took my license away, and it took me six months of well-placed ass-kissing to get it back. I would be more careful in the future.

There wasn't a lot of damage, and the car was fixed as good as new. Joan's hair grew over the cut, which helped ease my guilt, and the whole group went for a ride again with better results. However, Mom waited a little longer before she would ride with me. I guess she wanted a bit of a track record before she would tempt fate. Once in a while, Dad would borrow the Cadillac, and I would drive the station wagon. I called it the "social wagon" because I could get a bunch of people in it. The station wagon made for a hell of a deal on "Dollar Night" at the drive-in movies, when you could get in for a dollar a carload.

Blood Is Thicker than Wine

As kids went, I was a handful, but Jim was no day at the beach either. He gave my grandfather a run for his money. My grandfather thought Jim was the Antichrist. I wrote in an earlier story about my father's still and about my grandfather taking a swing at my father. Well, back when Jim was about sixteen years old, my grandfather had a wine cellar for his own use. He had about a dozen kegs of homemade wine that he shared with family and friends. The wine was affectionately known as "dago red" and was mighty tasty. Having homemade wine for your own use was not against the law. My grandfather drank wine with dinner, as did his father; it was a tradition.

Another tradition was playing bocce out in the yard and, of course, sipping a little wine while playing. My grandfather would invite his friends over to play botchy, a game played with balls about the size of coconuts. The bocce balls are rolled along the ground for about fifty feet, and there are positions where the balls could land to score points. A player could be in scoring position and could be knocked out by the ball of an opposing player, much like shuffleboard. These guys would play for hours and consume large amounts of "dago red." My uncle Alex, the oldest boy of the family, would fill the wine bottles when they got low. My grandfather had padlocks on the barrels, and only he and Alex had a key. My grandfather would not give Jim a key because, as my grandfather put it, "Jim learned to steal before he learned to walk."

Grand Pop was right. Jim learned to pick the locks on the kegs and was siphoning off each of the kegs so that the wine would not be missed and was selling it to the people in the neighborhood. That was not legal; that's bootlegging. Before my grandfather ever knew there was a shortage, the cops paid him a visit one Saturday night and told him that people in the neighborhood were getting drunk on wine from his cellar. Jim thought that when the old man found a shortage, he would automatically blame Alex. And because Alex was the number-one son, not much would happen to him. But Grand Pop didn't find the shortage; instead the cops came. Jim hadn't counted on this.

Grand Pop called Alex and, without asking him a thing, started to kick the living shit out of him. He beat him nonstop until he was tired of hitting him. Alex was a bloody lump lying on the living room floor. During the beating, Alex kept denying selling the wine. Every time he denied it, Grand Pop hit him more till Alex wised up and kept quiet. Jim said it was one of the worst beatings he had ever seen, and he had wanted to tell his father that he was the guilty one, but if this was what the favorite son got (and Jim being the least favorite), he thought his father would kill him. Jim waited until Grand Pop walked out of the room to approach Alex; he thought Alex was dead. He walked over to him and shook him, and Alex groaned. He was alive and Jim was relieved. Jim's conscience bothered him, but if he were to own up, he would get worse than Alex got, and Alex had already taken the rap, so Jim did the next best thing. He took some of the money he had made selling the wine and bought Alex off with a used car. Grand Pop never found out the truth about who sold the wine. The secret was kept. Blood is thicker than wine.

Hit in the Ass by the Number-Five Car

After reading the story about Jim and the wine he stole, you might think Jim always got away clean. Maybe he did get past my grandfather, but in life, as any realist will tell you, you pay now or you pay later, but you pay. In Jim's case it was later. He did not get a beating from my grandfather, but he got a beating. One night Jim and Mary were arguing, and while Jim was going out the door, Mom said, "I hope you get hit in the ass by a number-five car." This was a trolley car that ran through our neighborhood. Jim continued out the door and went to meet a friend whose name was Whiskey. (I don't know if that was a last name cut short or a nickname because he was a drinker. Jim with all his vices never drank, so I think it was a name cut short.) Jim was driving his panel truck that night, and Whiskey was the only passenger. There was no number-five car where Whiskey lived, but there was a number-three.

Mom got the call at about 10 PM: Jim and Whiskey were in the hospital. They had been stopped at a red light, and it had been raining heavily, and these trolley cars had steel wheels on steel tracks and were known to slide when wet. They had been hit in the ass by the number-three car: the curse had worked. Jim's panel truck was totaled. Almost all the bones in Whiskey's upper body had been broken, and Jim had broken his back. But both men recovered after a lengthy stay in the hospital.

Jim had back trouble for the next ten years. Amazingly, he got better as he got older, just the opposite of what's usually the case. Jim said that Mary put a curse on him and that she was a witch. Mom reminded Jim of the story about Alex and the wine and how Alex had taken that harsh beating for something Jim had done, and she told Jim, "The Lord moves in his own time!" Jim said, "Maybe so, but he don't need any help from you."

The Printing Press

For years Jim always complained he couldn't make enough money. Time after time, he said he needed a friggin' printing press to keep up with the family. He was right; we were a spoiled bunch of piranhas, and the more fish he threw in the tank, the more we ate. He never spent much on himself; his needs were simple. His only vice was gambling, and number one on the hit parade was horses. Even though he knew the odds were against him, he loved it! He said that when he lost, he was just being kind to dumb animals. When he won, he won big, and when he lost, he lost big. So Jim could have fifty thousand in his pocket one day and fifty cents the next, and his personality never changed; it just didn't bother him. The way he went through money, he really could have used a printing press.

As he got older, he spent more time around the house and stopped going out for three or four days at a time, but he would still stay out late. My mother was beginning to think that he was settling down, but then he started to stay out overnight again. My mother said to him, "What are you doing that you have to stay out all night?" Jim said, "Leave me alone. I'm makin' money." Now Jim claiming he was out all night making money was nothing new. He'd been saying that for years. My mother knew that during all those years he was staying out, it was never for another woman, unless she had four legs and could run six furlongs in fifty-eight and change.

Well, the staying out all night again lasted three months. Then to no one's surprise, guess who we saw on the late news. You're right, bad boy Jim. He wasn't lying; he really was making money—he got nailed for counterfeiting. Jim finally had gotten his printing press, and then the treasury guys confiscated it. He was making brand-spanking-new twenties. He had a station wagon full that he had planned to ship overseas. Jim had been under surveillance for some time, and in one fell swoop they got Jim, the plates, the press, and his boys. My mother had gotten a phone number where she could call to talk to Jim, to tell him about bail and so on. She had been here before and knew the drill, but she wanted to make sure that she didn't miss anything. She had me make the call; a man answered, and I said, "Do you have a James D'Angelo in custody?"

He said, "Hold on. Hey, Jim, it's for you." I could hear talking and laughing in the background. I could hear my father's voice. Then he picked up the phone and said hello, and I told him arrangements were being made to set bail and get him out. He said he was playing pinochle and got these guys "stuck" eighty bucks. He had talked them into gambling to pass the time. Yes, he was cheating the treasury men. It's hard to tell who had who captured. He said, "Take your time; these guys are easy, and I'll be coming home with real money." Then he said, "Take care of your mother," and hung up.

Eventually Jim's trial date rolled around, and Jim filled the courtroom with character witnesses. He had cops, clergy, politicians, bigwigs from the department stores (with whom he had contracts), and a fellow by the name of Preston Sharp (a bigwig in the Pennsylvania penal system). The judge sentenced him to probation and a fine of five thousand dollars. Jim replied, "How am I gonna pay five thousand? You guys took all my money." All Jim's friends in the courtroom roared. The judge put his hand in front of his mouth so that no one would see him laughing, Jim smiled at my mother, paid his fine, and was on to his next adventure.

Jim Carries His Ass Straight

At breakfast the morning after Jim's sentencing in the counterfeiting case, Mom and Dad were talking about the prior day's activities. Mom was really ragging on him. She said, "Did you finally learn your lesson, you incorrigible adult delinquent? It's only for the grace of God you're not in jail right now."

Jim was eating while reading a race sheet. He smiled and said, "Mary, you're right." My mother grinned from ear to ear. He looked up at the ceiling like he was thinking, looked back at my mother, and said, "I'm gonna carry my ass straight...for at least a week." And he went back to reading his race sheet.

Then my mother tried psychology: "What if you go to jail and get raped?" She thought this would have some impact on him.

Jim replied, "The screwing I'd get in jail can't be any worse than the screwing I'd get out here. They'd have to clothe, feed, and keep me for nothin'. It would be like a friggin' vacation." My mother shook her head and rolled her eyes and let out a light laugh.

It took only two visits from the probation officer before Jim had him meeting him at the track. Jim's cronies could barely believe this one. Who knows—Jim figured he might need him down the road for a character witness.

I Had a Creative Flair

At one point, Jim put his nose to the grindstone in his furniture business and caught up on some estimates that he needed to do. Jim would go out to a customer's home and give refinishing estimates, and he had a fine line of bullshit that would circle the globe. For example, we went out one day to give an estimate to refinish a bedroom suit (and keep in mind that Jim came highly recommended from prestigious department stores). The estimate went something like this. We were at a beautiful mansion on Philadelphia's mainline, and Jim rang the bell and a maid answered the door (the price of Jim's work, already high, went up when he saw they had a maid). Jim announced himself, and the maid went to get the lady of the house. Jim smiled at me with a devilish grin; he was in overcharge heaven.

The customer came into the room carrying a dog in her arms, and of course, Jim made a fuss over the pooch. Jim was laying the groundwork to knock her socks off with a huge price. She walked us upstairs to her bedroom. Jim complimented her on her wonderful taste and told her what a pleasure it was to be in such a beautifully decorated home. Actually, he didn't give a shit, but he was a great actor. He almost convinced me of his sincerity, as he maneuvered his prey with his wit and charm. He inspected the bedroom suite thoroughly, while telling the woman a humorous story about my mother and the two dogs we had at home, which was totally fabricated (I thought to myself, "What dogs?" but he was so explicit and the story was so funny that he had even me believing it).

After his inspection of the furniture, he asked her what kind of finish she would like. She said she didn't know, but she would like something new. She had just made a big mistake. Jim had a one-of-a-kind finish that he was going to do special for her. She couldn't wait to hear more. The finish he had in mind was a two-tone satin black base with white Formica top and brass drawer pulls (a finish that he'd actually done countless times before; he had black and white in half the bedrooms in the Philly area). He had noticed cigarette burns in her dresser top and told her that if he did the finish this way, she would not be able to burn this top or even hurt it with perfume spills. Then he went on to explain the difficulty and the intricacies of producing this fine black satin lacquer finish and integrating the Formica so as not to be noticed; he told her how her friends would envy her. He told her to close her eyes and imagine the contrast of the beautiful ornate brass drawer pulls glistening against a fine black satin lacquer finish.

Jim had her dancing on air, and before she could open her eyes, he had her agreeing to pay eight thousand dollars and not to bother him because it would take six to eight weeks to do the work. If she called or bothered him, he would send the furniture back. He said he would call and let her know when the work was completed. Actually, pickup and delivery and this type of finish could be done in less than a day's work. This was Jim's easiest finish to do and was a real moneymaker. As he told her, it would cost eight thousand dollars, and he said that she needed to give him four thousand dollars down and the balance on completion—and he'd appreciate it if she would give him a check right away; he was running late for another appointment. (Between you and me, the appointment he was talking about was getting to the bank to cash his check so that he could make the first race at Garden State Race Track.) This was in the late sixties, and it was not a bad day's pay.

He had done this black-and-white finish so many times that I knew his spiel word for word, and I could lip-sync along with him. One day, while giving another customer the same spiel, when he got to the part when he was going to say "black satin base with white Formica tops," he reversed it and said, "white satin base with black Formica tops." While the customer went to get her checkbook, Jim turned to me, standing on his toes and flicking his hair, and said, "I had a creative flair!" and it was a comical sight to say the least. He always told the customers it would take six to eight weeks to get their furniture back, but if he needed money, that time would be cut in half.

Moron Number One and Moron Number Two

You remember Barney, Jim's brother—you know, the comedian, the guy who never runs out of energy? Well, when Jim was catching up on his furniture work, Barney had time off from entertaining and was hanging around Jim's furniture-refinishing shop doing what Barney does best: singing, dancing, getting in the way, and breaking Jim's balls. Jim said, "Barney, you'd give an aspirin a headache." So to get rid of him, Jim was going to send him out on a furniture delivery with another eccentric, Frank Burkowitz, who wore a pencil-line mustache, suspenders, and bow ties and who combed his jet black hair straight back and fancied himself a singer. Frank worked for my father as an upholsterer. This dynamic duo Jim referred to as "Moron #1" (Frank) and "Moron #2" (Barney).

One day, when Barney was hanging around and pestering Jim to go to the racetrack, Jim sent Moron #1 and Moron #2 out on a delivery. Jim needed to deliver a sofa and chair that Frank had reupholstered, and there was nothing for Frank to do at the moment, so for peace and quiet, Jim thought it was a good idea to have Frank and Barney make the delivery. So they loaded the truck, and off they went on what should have been "a three-hour tour."

Five hours later, there was no sign of them, and Jim was getting concerned. He said, "I could have carried the sofa and chair on my back and done the delivery faster than these two morons!" So he made a call to the customer's home where the furniture was to be delivered. The phone rang, and a woman answered. Jim announced who he was and asked if the men had arrived there. She said, "Yes, several hours ago, and they're still here. "They're wonderful!" Barney was singing and dancing, telling jokes, juggling, and doing impersonations. Barney had done his entire stage act and sung a duet with Frank.

Jim, hearing this, asked the woman to have Moron #1 come to the phone. She started to laugh; she was amused by the whole thing. Jim could hear voices in the background. The woman said, "It's Mr. D'Angelo, and he wants to speak to Moron #1."

Frank said, "That's me!" and got on the line. Before Jim could utter a word, Frank told him how much fun it was working with Barney.

Jim interrupted Frank and said, "Get Moron #2, get in the truck and get back here on the double."

Frank, sensing Jim's abruptness, said, "Are you angry with us?"

Jim replied, "No, I'm lonely for you two assholes."

Frank held his hand over the phone and said to Barney, "Jim's mad at us."

The next voice on the line was Moron #2 (Barney) impersonating an old tough-guy movie actor, Jimmy Cagney: "All right, you dirty rat, I'm gonna give it to you the way you gave it to my sister. Bend over." They expected Jim to laugh, but there was only silence. Then Frank got back on the line, trying to misdirect Jim from his anger, and said that the woman loved the upholstery job and thought he and Barney were quite entertaining. Jim answered that Barney better get all the dancing out of his system because when they got back, Jim was going to tear off Barney's legs and beat Frank to death with the stumps. Then Jim hung up.

Sitting at his desk, Jim leaned back in his chair, laughing, and said to his office girl Rose, "My brother Barney's a fucking idiot."

Rose said, "What does that make you? You're laughing at him."

Jim said, "The brother of a fucking idiot," and Rose laughed.

About twenty minutes later, the truck pulled up, and out jumped Frank and Barney, laughing and grab-assing. Rose looking out the office window saw, them pull in, and yelled to Jim, who was working in the shop, "Martin and Lewis are here!"

Jim looked out the window and upon seeing that they were still clowning, turned to Rose and said with a smile on his lips, "No court would convict me." Then the door of the shop opened and in limped Frank and Barney like two bad teenagers. Jim said, "Did you vaudevillians remember to get paid for the upholstery job?" Frank handed Jim the check. Jim pinched their cheeks and said "Good boys"—end of story.

The Party at the Mansion

Jimmy D. took all problems with a grain of salt, and I helped add to those problems. Of course there was the time that I smashed up the Cadillac, and here's something else I did that could have given him an ulcer. My mother and dad went to see one of their horses running at an out-of-town track. When they went out of town, they were usually gone for three to four days. My sister and I would be in charge of the house and my two younger brothers. At this time, my sister Patsy was nineteen, I was sixteen, my younger brother Jimmy was ten, and brother Jerry was seven. Tony, the baby, went on the trip with them. They were to leave on a Thursday night and return on Monday.

It was near the end of the school year, and the weather was getting nice. We were living in the mansion on Roosevelt Boulevard in Philadelphia, and the colonial-style mansion had eight-foot hedges that surrounded the property, so it looked like an exclusive country club. The place was huge; you could park fifty to eighty cars on the lawn and there was enough room inside for hundreds of people. I decided in advance to have a party on the Saturday night they were gone. I knew three weeks ahead of time that my parents were going away, so I had three weeks to plan and work on the details.

Things went smoothly, and I invited everybody I knew from Lincoln High School, all over Philadelphia and the Northeast Village, and told them to invite everyone they knew. It was gonna be a chip-in party and was five dollars a head. There would be plenty of food, booze, and a live band. I had the guys from the school newspaper print up tickets for me (they were crude, but served the purpose). I collected the money for three weeks, and in the end I had a bundle. I bought seven half-kegs of beer and six cases of assorted booze and mixers, plates, cutlery, napkins, and so on. I had no trouble getting the food from the distributor. My buddy Frank McCann had the deepest voice, so he ordered it by phone. The distributor who had delivered here before for my father's parties brought it over. My sister's boyfriend was twenty-one, so he went out and bought the hard liquor.

I hired these two guys and a half a dozen more of my boys to check tickets when the people arrived. I had signs painted and stuck in the ground along the main highway for about two hundred yards that read, "This way to Bernie's Hideaway," and a sign at the driveway entrance with an arrow pointing up the driveway. This brought in strangers, but what the hell—if they could pay five bucks a head, they could stay. I also hired three girls to help me out in the kitchen. The kitchen was huge and very well-equipped. We laid out the food buffet style, and as fast as we could get it out, the people would eat it. I had told everyone it would be picnic style and to bring blankets. There was a staircase that spiraled around the main hall, and I stationed a couple of my boys at the bottom of the stairs to keep people from wandering through the house. There was another staircase from the kitchen, but that door had a lock, so that took care of that. The first floor was more than big enough to house all the people, and there were three bathrooms, so there was no reason for anyone to go upstairs.

About 7 PM people started to arrive, and at 8 PM the party was in full swing. Blankets were spread all over the lawn, and a lot of hugging and kissing was happening, especially in the spots where the floodlights couldn't reach. The band was playing, people were dancing, and everyone was reasonably well-behaved till about 11:30 PM, when these animals had drunk and eaten 98 percent of the food and booze. My sister said, "They're starting to get ugly." I had two hundred unappreciative drunks on my hands, and I was down to my last three hundred dollars. I needed to make a decision. I could spend what I had to shut them up, and that would keep them drinking and eating, but then I would have done the whole thing for nothing. It was time to take action. I made an anonymous phone call to the police and had the place raided. When the first squad car pulled up the driveway, people leaped through the hedges and ran down the back roads; just the sight of the cop car did the trick. Those who had cars parked behind the house took the driveway out. I never have seen a place clear out so fast.

I figured I was Jimmy D'Angelo's kid, and the cops wouldn't do anything but break up the party and report it to my dad. Then I'd have to make up a story for my dad and try to play it down. I figured I'd rather take my chances with him than try to cope with two hundred unruly drunks. I had a couple of days to clean up and make the place look like nothing had ever happened; plus I had three hundred bucks, and back then, three hundred bucks was a lot of money. Just then a set of headlights came up the driveway; it was the old man's car. They were home early—the horse was "scratched" (didn't race), and I was screwed. The place looked like a bomb had hit it; there were beer bottles and whiskey glasses all over the place, half-eaten plates of food, and even bits of clothing. It looked like a battlefield, and I was about to become its only casualty.

My mother got out of the car holding my baby brother Tony, and she had fire in her eyes. She looked at me the way she would look at Jim right before attacking him. My father told her to go into the house and said he would take care of me. She stormed into the house, but not without screaming and yelling at my father to kick my ass. By this time three more cop cars had pulled into the driveway. My father pointed at me and said, "You little prick, go to your room. I'll be in to straighten you out." He walked over to the driveway where the cops were, and I went up to my bedroom, where I could see the driveway from my window. The cops were laughing and shaking hands with the old man; this lasted about fifteen minutes, and then they left.

Jim came in the house, and my mother started yelling again, telling him what he should do to me. She wanted blood and lots of it, she said, and she screamed and hollered for what seemed to be forever. I thought my dad was losing the discussion, and I did not want to deal with my mother. Then there was silence. My sister stuck her head into my bedroom door and said, "You're dead!" as if she was telling me something I didn't know. She went back into her room, and I heard footsteps on the stairs. My bedroom door opened, and there was Jim, very calm. I couldn't tell if he was very, very angry or just very angry. Either way, it didn't look good. He shut the door behind him and locked it. I thought, *Well, I made it to sixteen.* I figured he locked the door because he didn't want any witnesses.

He walked over to me and said, "The truth, tell me the truth. What went on here tonight?" I told him everything—how long I had planned it, how much money I had made, and how I called the cops to get rid of the drunks so that I could keep the three hundred. He took off his belt and folded it in half, and the blood drained from my head—and then he started to beat the living shit out of the furniture. He said, "Yell, cry, make your mother think I'm killing you." He hit the bed, he hit the walls—he hit anything that would make a loud slap. He said, "When I leave, keep moaning, but not too much." I got into bed, and he walked to the door, unlocked it, turned, and looked at me and said, "You're a chip off the old block," and then he smiled and turned off the light.

But I didn't get away without being punished. The next day Jim got me out of bed at 6 AM to clean the house and the grounds. I got dressed and went downstairs and started to pick up all the trash. While I was cleaning up, my mother walked in, and she still was breathing flames. She went wild all over again, and Jim heard the yelling and came into the kitchen. He had a plan to shut her up. He knew my mother wanted the house painted. Jim said to me, "You're not going to see your friends, so tell them not to come around. You're grounded for life, and you're not gonna sit around just doing nothin'. You're going to paint the house!"

This got my mother off my case for the moment; she was beaming. She would get the house painted, and I was getting punished. She was a happy little mother. It would take at least two to three weeks of sunup-to-sundown work, the mansion being so large with a huge double-wide carport, a four-car garage, and columns in the front of the house that stood from the porch floor to the third-floor roof. I scraped and painted for half the summer. After the first couple of weeks, Mom stopped ragging, but I was still doing the job under her close scrutiny. I would have preferred an ass-kicking, which proves the old saying "crime don't pay" (when you get caught).

Grandpop Jim

Over the years, all of us tried Jim's patience. He never hit one of us or rarely even looked at us in anger; however, when we grew up and had children of our own, and we'd complain about our kids giving us crap, he'd just smile and say, "Isn't parenthood wonderful?" My sister Pat and I were the first to have kids, and they loved Grandmom and Grandpop. Jim always talked to the kids like they were adults; because of this, I believe, they became responsible and felt like equals in the family at a young age. This was a good thing. Jim yelled and screamed at everybody, including the kids. You would think this would make the kids nervous, but no, kids and animals know when you love them.

My sister Patsy had two girls (Robin and Diane), and I had two boys (Bernie and Vince). They played together often at their grandparents' house. They were very close to each other and their grandparents, and they weren't afraid of Jim's loud voice. If he yelled too much, they would say, "Oh Grandpop, be quiet!"

He'd say to my mother, "Do you believe these little bastards telling me to be quiet?"

She would always side with the kids and say, "Then shut your big dago yap."

Now Jim would act insulted and say, "I don't get any respect from you assholes," and jump into his car and head for the poolroom (just an excuse to stick Mom with the kids while he played with his cronies). Sometimes he'd take the kids with him; actually, he did this a lot. He'd feed them pizza and soda and teach them how to play pool, and they'd hang for hours. He always brought them home exhausted, but happy. Grandpop gave them, like all of us, a lot of attention, and because he was so popular, the kids felt important. Jim always figured out a way to include you in what he was doing, even if you were only six years old.

The Hex of the Witch

Everything in Jim's life didn't always run smoothly. He had ups and downs in both legal and illegal business, and when things went bad, he would sell everything in sight to stay afloat. In his words, he was "balls to the wall," and he sold something that he would regret for more reasons than one. What he did was sell Fuente, the horse that had made him a bundle and that my mother loved deeply. She found out from Jim's trainer, Dave Ginsberg, who called the house to tell Jim that the sale went OK. Jim wasn't there to get the phone, and my mother picked it up. Now Jim always thought my mother was a witch, and what happened next was the icing on the cake. My mother said, "You sold the goose that laid the golden egg. You'll never make another dollar."

No matter how much Jim tried to explain how necessary it was and that he waited till it was absolutely necessary before selling Fuente, his explanations fell on deaf ears. Well, after Mom said "you'll never make another dollar," Jim's furniture business went into the red for the first time in twenty-five years, the horses he had left stopped winning and he had to sell all of them, and for the next three years everything he touched turned to shit. Mom had a hex on him (pretty spooky stuff). In time Jim eked his way out of the hole and back in the black and was on top once again. He said it was the worst hex the witch ever put on him.

Jim's Dental Plan

Jim took care of a lot of people, but the one person he neglected was himself. He never went to a doctor, and Mom had to beat him to go to the dentist. He was complaining about his teeth, and he kept putting off going to the dentist; he put it off till the pain got so bad he couldn't stand it. Finally, after several sleepless nights, he agreed to get checked out. I think that "Mr. Fearless" was less than enchanted with drills and other tools of torture used by the tooth fairy. Well, when he came back, he was full of Novocain, and he had relief from the pain for the first time in days. My mother said, "Now was that so bad?"

He replied, "I'm going back tomorrow and get them all pulled." The dentist had said he needed a costly makeover—root canal, caps, the works—and Jim was not going to spend the time and money.

Mom said, "You don't have the balls to get all your teeth pulled," and laughed. She didn't take him seriously. The next day, Jim went to the dentist. The whole family knew what he had said, but no one believed it. But at about five o'clock in the evening, in walked Jim, balls in place, but not a tooth in his head. Shortly after, Jim got fitted for his winning smile, uppers and lowers, which he carried around in his sweater pocket. Dad never was a slave to fashion.

The Mob Olympics
(The Footrace at the Track)

Even as Jim got older, he didn't slow down; he still played like he was a kid. He made things fun. When a gang of us (Jim and his cohorts) would go to the track, he would park in the furthest parking spot from the building. Then Jim and his merry men would have a footrace to the main admissions booth, and the last man there would have to pay the entrance fee for everyone. These races were classics. The contestants were out-of-shape, mostly overweight, nonathletic hoods who dressed more like pimps than track stars. The slower runners got the usual head start, and that's as fair as it got. Once the race got underway, there was pushing, shoving, holding, biting, and making shortcuts between parked cars, not to mention the name-calling and cursing. These guys were more fun to watch than the horses. Some could only make it halfway. The guys that were in better shape would stop, look back, and taunt them, saying things like "You run like the stiffs [the horses] that you bet on." The slower, out-of-breath guys, fighting off cardiacs while leaning on Pontiacs and gasping for air, would hurl profanities as well as an occasional shoe at their stable mates. Jim was fat with skinny legs, but he could run like a deer. He always finished up front, except one day when he was in full gallop when he realized he'd left his car running and the keys locked inside. This got big laughs from the boys along with some remarks that were less than complimentary. Jim could take it as well as well as give it out. The boys asked him what he was going to do about the situation. He gave his stock answer—"Fuck it"—and went on into the racetrack.

The Race between Young Jim and Old Jim

Jim didn't just race the older guys; he also raced my brother Jimmy who had just gotten home from Vietnam and was all bone and muscle, young, and in great shape (my old man loved the challenge). Jim was always saying how none of his boys would make a pimple on his ass, and when young Jimmy heard this, he took him to task. They started two blocks from the house, about three hundred yards. It was a straight run to the street where we lived, and then a left turn about thirty yards in front of our house to the finish line. My brothers Jerry and Tony and I were the spectators, and much to our surprise, for the first hundred yards they looked to be neck and neck. Jim had his fat ass in high gear, but he didn't know young Jim had another gear, and young Jim started pulling away. As they approached the turn to the house, young Jim had a clear lead. When old Jim decided to cut across our neighbor's lawn, this cut off a huge chunk of the course. They were close to even again. But the neighbor had the sprinklers on, and old Jim started slipping and sliding and lost his footing and finished on his back, sliding across our driveway, declaring himself the winner. However, this was not the case. Even so, young Jim, knowing how competitive the old man was and how much he loved to cheat, did the sonly thing and agreed that the old man had won. After all, the truth was he had just gotten beaten by a pimple on his ass.

Everyone's Got a Price

On the other side of the coin, there's my sister Patsy. Patsy attended a private school at the request of my mother. Although Patsy was very intelligent, a straight-A student, she was not always a saint at Saint Mary's Academy for Girls. Don't get me wrong—she wasn't bad, just highly spirited. Well, one day it was her turn to test Jim's ability to handle people. She got suspended and needed a parent to go to the school to get her reinstated, and knowing my mother would beat her unconscious, she needed to get back in school before my mother found out. This meant Jim had to talk to the Mother Superior. Anyone who went to Catholic school will tell you they don't call them "mothers" for nothing. They're not easy to deal with to say the least.

I don't remember what Patsy did to get her ass in a jam, but knowing my sister, I bet it was creative. She was always thinking and maneuvering (wonder where she got it). Well, the morning they went to the school to meet the Mother, Jim had something up his sleeve. Walking to the car, Patsy said, "I don't think they'll let me back in school." Jim said, "Don't worry. I'll take care of it." Pulling up to the school, they got out of the car and walked into the office of the Mother Superior, the head penguin. Jim introduced himself and by the time they finished exchanging pleasantries, Jim had already sized her up and started off with a soothing line of bullshit that held the nun's attention. But before he moved in for the kill, he asked if he could talk to her in private and, with her permission, put Patsy way outside the office. The nun complied, and Patsy walked out of the room.

Jim had a canvas bag under his arm (or I should say up his sleeve). In the bag were two silver candleholders that he offered to donate to the school; they were beautiful (not to mention hot—he had fenced them the day prior). Fifteen minutes later, the door opened up, Jim was laughing, Mother Superior was laughing, and Patsy was back in school. In all, it was not a bad morning's work. St. Mary's received stolen goods, Patsy got reinstated, and my mother never found out. Patsy asked how he got her reinstated so fast as he lit a cigarette and put it between his teeth, in the center of his mouth. Taking a super long drag, blowing it out both sides of his mouth, he winked at her and said, "Kid, everybody's got a price, even God's little helpers."

PART III

The Mechanic

You know, hanging out with Jim and the boys, it was hard to keep my nose out of Jim's business. I wanted to go to a card game and sit in as a shill or learn to be a "mechanic" (someone who can manipulate cards). My dad had me practice for about a year till I could do what was needed in a game to win the money.

One of the things I learned was how to "move a cooler." I may have mentioned what a cooler is but I'll refresh your memory. A cooler is when you take a deck of cards and stack them, giving a great hand to the "mark" (the person you're going to win the money from) and the winning hand to a shill (one of our guys). The stacking takes place before the game starts. The preset deck or decks were kept in my suit coat pockets so that I could take one out whenever needed.

These decks could be brought into the game several ways. One way is to have a deck that was steamed open from the bottom and the plastic wrapper slid off. Then the cards were arranged and put back in and the plastic wrapper was resealed. During the game, one of the shills would ask for a new deck when it was my turn to deal. Now I would tear open a new deck, throw aside the jokers and false-shuffle, making it look like the cards were being mixed when in fact they were not. Then they were set in front of a shill to my right to be cut. He would false cut or simply refuse to cut, and then the preset hand would be dealt. Another method is to sit to the right of the mark, and when he asks you to cut, that's when the switch is made. It's a sleight-of-hand move and very difficult, but very effective because the mark deals his own demise; he deals the preset hands. The marks never know what hits them.

Well, my first time out, this is what the mob wanted me to do. I was sitting with Jim and four mobsters and one mark loaded with money that he thought he was going to take to the casinos in Atlantic City. But the boys had a better idea; they were going to save him the drive from Philly to AC (how thoughtful). Well the game started, and everything was going smoothly; on the surface it looked like a legitimate game. Then about fifteen or twenty minutes in, I got the signal to make the move. It was a no-limit game, which means you can bet as much as you like. This could break the mark in one hand. I was seated to the right of the mark, and I was to do the sleight of hand and false-cut the preset deck and let the mark deal the bomb. But instead I froze and just cut the cards. The mobsters just looked at me. I guess they figured I would make the move the next time the deal came around.

Well, the deal came around the second time, and my heart was in my mouth. The mark looked right at me and said, "Cut." I froze for the second time!

A mob guy sitting next to me whispered, "What's wrong?"

I said, "The mark stares at me. What if he makes me?"

The guy said, "What's he gonna do when we're here?"

That was a good point; I was sitting with killers. Then he made a second point; he said, "If you don't make the move the next time around, I'm going to shoot you. I don't lose any fuckin' money ever!"

Well, no one had ever explained it like that before. So the next time around, with the mark looking at me and me sweating marbles and sporting a nervous grin, I made the move. The ice was broken; we won the money. When the game was over, we went to an Italian restaurant in South Philly and had a late dinner. The boys congratulated me; as they put it, I "broke my cherry." My dad and the boys had a good laugh at the greenhorn. I had a new respect for hustlers. Now when they said my dad pissed ice water, I knew what they meant. Believe me, it looks easy in the movies, but real life is different.

Jim said, "I'm proud of you, son. You were a little slow coming out of the gate. You just needed a little nudge."

I said, "A little nudge? These guys were going to shoot me."

He laughed and said, "They wouldn't shoot you."

I replied, "No?"

Jim said, "No, if you didn't make the move, I'd have shot ya."

Then everybody laughed, and Jim put his arm around me and said, "You're my kid, and no one would hurt you. They knew you needed a little help to get you going, and it worked."

The Night Watchman

One time Jim, actually took a job. Jim hadn't had a job working for someone other than himself since he was twenty. The reason Jim decided to become gainfully employed will be apparent once I fill you in on the details. One of his friends was building a house in the country, and at the same time, Jim took a job as a night watchman at a construction site where they were building expensive single homes. You guessed it—Jim's a builder, and only the best for Jim's buddies. Jim had a trailer with a cot, a TV, and a phone. With the phone in the trailer, Jim's friends could call to see when the coast was clear (Dracula was watching the blood bank). To make a long story short, they cleaned out the site. The only thing left was Jim and his trailer. They took everything they needed, every board, every nail, roofing supplies, and the like—about a trailer load or more. The next morning, Jim called the cops and reported the theft and then called his boss. When his boss got to the site and saw that everything was gone, he fired Jim on the spot. Jim was about sixty-six years old and a great actor. He'd have had an Academy Award if given the opportunity to steal one. He begged for his job, and his eyes teared up, and his quivering voice was so convincing that his boss started to reconsider. (Jim liked to shit. Jim didn't want to work; his job was done.) His boss said, "You fell asleep on the job, and I can't take a chance on you again." Jim said doggedly that he understood, and he lowered his head and walked away, out of a job, but in the lower-than-wholesale building-supply business.

Jim's Prostate Operation

As the years went on, Jim never mellowed, and he kept his youthful energy. When he walked into a room, he filled it with that energy. He exhibited this when he was going into the hospital to undergo tests and have an operation on his prostate. As Jim put it, his shut-off valve wasn't working. When he would finish urinating, he would zip up, and an annoying dozen or so drips would continue. He said he needed a plumbing overhaul. He said he was tired of pissing his pants and standing in a public restroom shaking his dick till the drip stopped. He said it looked like he was playing with himself, and he didn't want to make the net (get locked up), as he put it, for playing with his pump gun in a public restroom. He said it would look bad on his resume of arrests.

So he entered Abington Hospital. The following day, my sister Pat and I were driving over to visit him. On the way, we were discussing how active Jim was and how he loved his freedom and was not much for rules and regulations, like the dos and don'ts that hospitals have. He had always made his own rules. We thought this would be pure torture. Wow, were we wrong! Arriving at the hospital, we went to the information desk. Behind the desk was an elderly, sophisticated-looking woman with a calm, almost quiet voice. We asked her what room James D'Angelo was in. Without going to the registry to look it up, she said loudly and clearly "305." She lost her quiet voice and said "Are you friends or relatives?"

I said, "Son and daughter."

"Oh, it's a pleasure to meet you," she responded. "He's the talk of the hospital. He's so funny that he keeps everyone in stitches. When you see him, tell him Gail said hello. If I get a chance, I'll stop up for a few minutes."

I thought to myself, *He is only here one day and he's already on a first-name basis.* Gail directed us to the elevator, waving and smiling at us as the doors closed. We pushed the button for the third floor, and when we reached the floor, the doors opened, and we stepped off. But instead of looking for the number markings on the wall to indicate which way 305 was, we followed loud voices and laughter. We walked past an empty nurse's station to the first room, 305. Usually, a patient is allowed three or four visitors, but there were about ten people in the room, and half were friends and half were nurses. Everyone was laughing; it looked like a party.

Jim was sitting in a chair next to his bed. People were sitting on his bed, on the spare chair, and on the windowsills surrounding him. As Pat and I walked into the room, Jim was talking, but he spotted us and stopped mid-sentence and said, "Bernie, Pat, come on in and join the rest of us. Sit down and make yourself miserable!" He introduced us as his kids. Everyone said what a pleasure it was having him in the hospital; he was making it a pleasure to come to work. Then a male nurse came into the room. Jim looked up and said, "Do you have it?"

The man replied, "Does the Pope wear a dress?" From the sound of the nurse's voice, his mannerisms, and the way he walked, he was gay and proud of it.

He had brought my father the *Morning Telegraph* (which included a racing form that had the next day's entries from racetracks in Maryland, New York, Pennsylvania, and Delaware). The room was full of laughter, and Jim was the center of it. He had been there one day and had the run of the place. Ken was already running errands for him, and for this Jim promised to make him a handicapper. A handicapper is someone who takes information about horses that is printed in newspapers like the *Morning Telegraph* and picks winners. The Telegraph gives information like such as when and where the horses ran last (actually the last five times or so), whether they won or what position they finished, who rode them, and what track, and about a hundred other variables. No self-respecting horse degenerate would be caught without his *Morning Telegraph*, and no small thing like having his prostate scraped and undergoing a battery of tests was going to stop Jim from doing what comes naturally: trying to beat the odds.

The people in the room started going back to their duties, and eventually, it was just Jim, Pat, and I. Just before we were ready to leave, as we were putting on our coats, Ken returned to the room. We were saying goodbye, and Ken pulled a chair up to the bed and said a few nice things about Jim. Jim smiled and said, "I'm going to get rid of your mother, and I'm gonna marry her," pointing to Ken.

Ken laughed and said, "What makes you think I'd have you, you big pain in the ass?"

Then in a feminine voice, Jim replied, "Ooo, don't get sexy in front of the kids."

Ken replied, "Shut your face and read the race sheet. Pick some winners, or you'll have to find another errand girl."

Jim looked at Pat and me and said, "Never let them know you care." They were poking fun at each other, but Ken would get the last laugh because of Jim's condition. Over the next few days of testing, Jim would need several enemas, and Ken was the man for the job. The day that Jim got his last enema, Pat and I were just walking into the room. Jim was sitting on the edge of his bed, and shaking his head, he looked at us and said, "I came into this whorehouse a he-man, and I'm going out a fagot."

Ken laughingly looked at Pat and me and said, "He's incorrigible, but a hell of a lot of fun." Then Ken smiled and left the room and went on to his other duties.

When Jim talked, his voice carried, and the girls at the nurse's station were eavesdropping and were laughing hysterically about the carryings-on between him and Ken. Jim, hearing them laugh, said, "Go ahead and laugh! What kind of place is this? I just got raped and you're all laughing." This made them laugh even harder. The other patients on the floor were also laughing hysterically.

The nurses at the nurse's station said, "He goes from room to room visiting, and you know where he is by following the laughter as he makes his rounds." His talent for winning over people was put to good use during his stay. The morning of his release, the people who worked on the floor—doctors, nurses, janitorial help, and volunteers—were there to see him off; they had a little going-away party for him. They expressed how much they had enjoyed meeting him and wished him well.

Then Ken gave him a big hug, and Jim said, "Bern, get me out of here before he knocks me up."

Ken, giggling with his hand over his mouth, looked at me and said, "He's a treasure."

We get on the elevator with Jim in a wheelchair (he was fine; the wheelchair was protocol). He felt great, his doctor had fixed his leak, and Ken had gotten him regular. I asked him how he felt and he said "like a new woman". And home we went.

Dinner at Bookbinders
(A Philly Landmark)

I told you the story about Jim getting all of his teeth pulled and how he almost never had his false teeth in his mouth. He kept them in his back pants pocket and said that when he sat down, they'd bite him on the ass, and that's the closest he was getting those days to kinky sex. He said he only kept them for eating, which brings me to the story at hand. One night, Jim, my brother Gerry, my uncle Frank, my uncle Barney, and I were hanging around the poolroom, and nothing much was happening; things were pretty slow (no one to hustle or con, not even a card game in the back room). We were in hustler's hell: a state of boredom. Then out of the blue, Jim said, "I feel like eating fuckin' lobster. I'm gonna call Bookbinders and get us a table."

My uncle Barney, who being notoriously cheap would only part with money to bet on horses, said, "Are you out of your fuckin' mind? Do you know how expensive that place is?"

Then my uncle Frank chimed in: "It costs an arm and a leg and I only got one leg!"

Jim replied "I'm buying, you cheap cocksuckers." The boredom was over. They couldn't get their coats on fast enough. We were on a mission. We were going to dine in a Philadelphia landmark. We had about a fifteen- to twenty-minute ride from northeast Philly to center city. As usual, Barney was singing and telling jokes and doing impersonations of movie stars. He kept everybody laughing, so the whole trip seemed like only five minutes.

We pulled up to the valet parking. Gerry, Barney, and I were sitting in the back of the car, and Jim was driving. Uncle Frank was sitting in the front passenger seat with his crutches to his left standing up and leaning against the seat from floor to ceiling. As the valet opened the door on the passenger side, Uncle Frank turned to his left to grab his crutches, and Barney tried to climb out of the car from the backseat over Frank's shoulders. We had just pulled up to the fanciest place in town, and the boys were acting up already. Barney was yelling, "I'm starving!"

This pissed off Frank, and he started in: "You simple-looking cocksucker! Jim, get a load of this simple-minded prick. He's like a little kid." While trying to push Barney back, Frank continued, "When I get out of the fucking car, I'm gonna wrap my fucking crutch around your head, you crazy bastard." Then, hollering at Jim, Frank said, "Your father's to blame; he should have shot this prick at birth." Frank's face was blood red from yelling, his veins were popping out of his neck, and his blood pressure must have been off the chart. The guy holding the door was laughing uncontrollably, and people entering the restaurant were peering. I believe they were less than enchanted to see the animals with which they were about to share this evening's dining experience. Bon appétit.

Barney was now out of the car and tap dancing and singing show tunes. My brother Gerry was bent over with laughter, looking at me while laughing and talking at the same time: "And it's just the shank of the evening," Gerry said. Shaking his head, he said, "No one would believe this."

I said, "We're out with the world's oldest juvenile delinquents."

As we all headed for the front door of the restaurant, Barney was imitating the cowardly lion from Wizard of Oz, asking Frank, "Do ya wanna fight?" This made Frank stop the profanities and laugh. Jim, bringing up the rear, said, "All right now, you assholes behave." Truth was he enjoyed their actions as much as we did. The boys were out to have fun and were having it. We entered the restaurant. The maitre d' asked if we had a reservation, and Jim gave a name that I'd never heard before, which was normal. These guys never would make a reservation in their own names.

The maitre d' started to walk us to our table. Frank said to Jim—in a quiet voice for the first time in his life—using a lot of facial expression, "Before the dinner's over, I'm gonna kill this crazy bastard." This meant there was more fun ahead. This started Gerry laughing again. For some unexplainable reason everyone was gaping at us. When we reached the table, I figured so far so good. We started to pull up our chairs, and Barney and Frank were like four-year-olds poking fun at each other.

Jim reprimanded them both like a father figure as the waiter came to our table and asked, "Would you like a drink?"

Frank said, "What do you have that will make me forget this guy?" while pointing his finger at Barney.

Barney was about to open his mouth when Jim stepped in and said affectionately, "Both of you, shut the fuck up. The next one who opens his mouth, I'm gonna stick my fork in his throat." This quieted the kids for now. The waiter was holding back a laugh. I'm sure he was more accustomed to good manners and pleasantries of the normal clientele. This group was anything but normal. He seemed to enjoy our company. If nothing else, we broke the monotony. Jim did not drink alcohol, and oddly enough, neither did Barney. I couldn't even imagine what Barney would be like drinking. The tough guys all ordered soda, and my brother Gerry and I shared a bottle of merlot.

While we were waiting for our drinks we were perusing the menu. This place was known for its whole lobster. The waiter returned with our drinks, and we were ready to order. The lobster was very pricey, and the vegetables and sides were à la carte, but what the hell—Jim was paying. The waiter started with Uncle Frank. He ordered lobster and vegetables, and so did everyone else till it was Jim's turn. He ordered two lobster dinners.

The waiter said "Two lobster dinners? These lobsters are huge. Are you sure you can eat them both?"

Jim reached in his back pocket, pulled out his dentures and set the tops on the bottoms on the edge of the table (it looked like the table was smiling), and said, "Bring one lobster for me and one for him," pointing to the smiling dentures.

This cracked the waiter up. By some miracle we got through dinner, with Gerry and me laughing, with Frank talking several octaves above a shout, with Barney doing his James Cagney impersonations and talking to his lobster tail, and with Jim repeatedly telling them to shut the fuck up. It was a miracle they didn't throw us out. Now we just had to survive the ride home. As we left the restaurant, the maitre d' gave a sigh of relief. I said to Jim while we were waiting for our car, "Do you think they'll let us back in again?"

Smiling, he gave his stock answer: "Fuck em." We were no longer hungry or bored. We got into our car and headed home.

When Pat Tied the Knot

When my sister announced she was going to get married, it was a shock. Although she had been dating the same guy for about a year, there wasn't any talk of marriage. Her boyfriend's name was Charlie Rillara. Charlie was of Filipino and German extraction, and he looked 100 percent Hawaiian. I bring this up because my father had a nickname for everyone. Charlie's nickname was Sabu (Sabu was the name of a character in stories that took place in the jungle). Although he was never mistaken for Sabu, Charlie was taken for Don Ho, a Hawaiian singer popular in the late 1950s or early 1960s. When this would happen, Charlie would tell people he was Don Ho's brother Hanna. This meant he was "Hanna Ho," and this was before Pee Wee Herman. Charlie went as far as to have cards made up with a picture of a Hawaiian fire dancer with a muscular physique and wearing a loin cloth. Then Charlie superimposed his head on the body and had his name printed on it ("Hanna Ho"). So when people asked him if he was Don Ho, he would tell them he was his brother and hand them a card. He had a great sense of humor and was maybe a little nuts, so he fit right in with the D'Angelos.

Although his nickname was Sabu, most everyone called him Charlie, except Jim on the occasions when he'd be looking for him. Then it was "Has anyone seen Sabu?" or once in a while, he'd refer to him as the elephant boy. I personally always thought he looked like a 1950s movie actor, Tony Curtis. Jim liked Charlie, and the feeling was mutual. As a matter of fact, the whole Rillara family was a pleasant addition.

Getting back to the wedding, there seemed to be some emphasis on time. Pat was multiplying herself, and from what Pat had told me, she was not sexually active, well not the big nasty. But when she gave it a try, bingo beginner's luck. When she broke the news to Jim, he said, "That's what you get when you play hide the pineapple." I guess that's the Hawaiian version of "hide the salami." I didn't know how my mother took the news, but I'm sure not as easy as Jim. As long as Pat was happy, Jim was happy. He simply said, "You can't stop the world from going around, so on with the wedding."

Pat was only nineteen, and she got married July 12 and went on her honeymoon, but was back July 13. They said it wouldn't last—more "agida" for the old man. He had given them a sizable wedding gift in the form of a check and said that Pat was home before the ink was dry. Now his daughter was back home, she was six months pregnant, Mom was pissed off, and Jim was in the middle; everything was normal.

On their wedding day, Charlie had been over an hour late, and we thought he had second thoughts, but this was not the case. The longer we knew Charlie, the more we understood that he was late for everything. He took longer to get dressed than my sister; to say the least he was meticulous and tidy, and over the years this drove everyone nuts. When Jim would take Charlie to the track, and post time was one o'clock, Charlie would start getting ready about 7 AM. It took him so long to do things that I wondered how my sister got pregnant. If it took that long to get dressed, how long did it take him to get undressed? Pat must have been very patient. Pat would show her patience twice, once with the firstborn, Robin, and her second-born, Diane, who grew up to be beautiful young ladies who could get dressed faster than their father. Pat, Charlie, and the girls lived around the corner from Jim and Grandma Mary, which was a frequent hangout for the whole gang. These were good days!

Mom the Landscaper

I didn't mention in the last story about how Pat got her engagement ring. Jim got it for her from a guy that dealt in jewelry, specializing in diamonds. Back then, two and a half carats of excellent quality cost about eight thousand dollars, and Charlie paid twelve hundred. The guy that got it for them was affectionately called Joe the Jew by all the mobsters, a stocky, red-faced, cigar-smoking, happy-go-lucky soul who bought from burglars and sold to the public, sometimes back to the original owners. Jim and Joe had been friends since they were kids and socialized a lot together. Joe liked to go to Chinese restaurants, so Joe and his wife and Jim and Mary would over the years try all the Chinese restaurants in Philly's Chinatown. Joe liked to drink, and when he had too many, he would squint his eyes, show his top teeth, and pretend to talk Chinese. It's hard to put on paper how comical he looked and sounded, but he'd even crack up the Chinese waiters. When it came time to pay the bill, Jim would tell the waiter, "Give it to the Jew prick; he's buying." However, if Joe saw the waiter coming with the bill first, he'd say "Give it to that dago prick; he's buying!" They weren't politically correct, they didn't have to be; they were friends. And this was a friendship that was impenetrable for over sixty years. I notice that all the sharpies and frauds had long-term marriages and friendships, and this is not what most people would expect; it does make you think.

One summer morning, Joe and Jim went out to do some business about 8 AM. About 9 AM, a large dump truck came down our street. There were three men sitting in the truck. It stopped, and two of the men got out. They each took a separate side of the street and went door to door. They were trying to sell the truck's contents. They had a truckload of pig shit they were trying to sell as fertilizer. When they got to our house, my mother answered the door. They told her they had a truckload of the best fertilizer money could buy. Mom asked how much and the guy replied "$200." On today's market, that would be over a thousand dollars.

Mom gave the OK, and the men covered our front and back lawn in pig shit three inches deep. They said it was the end of the load, so she got extra. Mom got a deal. The smell—no, the stench—was unbelievable, and it made my eyes water.

As a matter of fact, it made the whole neighborhood's eyes water. The calls started to come over the phone, and the comments were less than enchanting. My mother's resolve was unshakable; she simply told everyone who didn't like it to kiss her big Irish ass. Mom was beautifying her lawn and giving it all the healthy luster that only a ton and a half of pig shit could do. The calls ceased; they figured they'd wait for Jim to get home, and they'd deal with him because he could be reasoned with.

The sun was directly overhead, the pig shit was beginning to boil, and the stench was at its peak when Jim pulled up in front of the house with Joe. They looked at each other as if to say, "Did you shit yourself?" As they got out of the car, Jim realized he was the proud owner of a ton and a half of pig shit, maybe three quarters because Mom got extra. What a deal. Jim stood there getting the full blast of the sun-baked shit. Joe put on his Chinese face and said, "Ooo something stinky. Me thinky someone shitty on lawny." I came out of the house to meet them.

Jim looked at me and said, "What the fuck is this?"

I replied, "It's pig shit. It's good for the lawn."

He rolled his eyes and ran his fingers through his hair and said in a very tight voice, "Do we have pigs?"

I said, "No."

He said, "Oh good, do you mind telling me how this shit got here?"

I said, "Mom bought it off a truck driver."

He barked, "Bought it?!" His eyes rolled up again in his head, and he said, "How much?"

I said, "$200."

Now he was rocking back and forth on his heels while surveying his newly fertilized property, and he took out a cigarette, lit it, and finished it with only three deep drags, and then went into the house. Joe was still talking Chinese saying "Stinky poo" and looked at me laughing. Jim walked into the kitchen, and Mom was there having tea with Patsy and a neighbor, Peggy Hartley. Peggy was a good neighbor and loved the adventure that Jim and Mary brought to the neighborhood. Jim said, "Good afternoon, girls," and with a smirk said, "What's new?"

Mom snapped back, "Don't get smart, you ignorant Dago. For your information, I'm fertilizing the lawn." Mom was prepared to stand by her work. Jim knew he was faced with many problems. One, how to get all the shit off the lawn; two, where to dump it; three, how to kill the remaining smell; and four, how to do one, two, and three without making Mom mad. Pat and Peggy were giggling, and this wasn't helping matters. Jim asked Mom how much she paid for it, and she said "$200."

He said, "That's a lot of shit for only $200" and then said, "They laid it on a little heavy." He was going to scrape some of it off and share it with Joe. Joe knew not to say a word; he knew Jim was looking for an opening to get this stuff cleaned up. It was a good thing Mom wasn't thinking because Joe lived in a high rise in center-city Philadelphia. Unless he was going to spread it all over the lobby, he had no use for it. Mom wanted to go food shopping, so I took her. She was out of the house, but Dad had to move fast. He got one of his construction buddies to come with a truck, and they shoveled it up and watered the lawn trying to kill the stench. We didn't know what was in the so-called fertilizer, but it was on the ground for not even a day and over the next week our grass was dying. We were instructed to never talk about it again in front of Mom. Dad said, "Your Mom put the whore in horticulture," shook his head, got in his car, and went to the poolroom. Tension was tight for a few days, but as the smell went away, so did the memory of Mom's days as a landscaper.

While the Cat Slept,
the Mice Played

Although Mom's intentions were innocent and she was the victim of a fast-talking shit salesman, in this next story she's anything but innocent. One day, Mom, Aunt Clara, and Aunt Francis (all friends from childhood) were sitting in our living room in an apartment at 2071 East Clearfield Street in Philadelphia. I was home from school sick, but I was feeling pretty good and had nothing to do, so I was hanging around with the women (probably being annoying) when Jim came home after being out all night gambling. He was visibly exhausted from lack of sleep. He walked in the front door and greeted the ladies with not a customary hello, but a smile, and said, "What are you whores up to?"

Aunt Clara answered him and said, "Jim, kiss my ass!"

Jim responded, "I'm too tired. I'm going to bed," and walked to the last room in the apartment, which was a bedroom, so that he would be furthest from the girls and have peace and quiet. He took off his clothes ands dropped them where he stood and dove into the bed. Within seconds he was snoring away. Considering the contented smile on his face, he must have won money gambling, and now he was dreaming about it. He lay there dead to the world.

Meanwhile, back in the living room, Mom and the girls were talking about how tired and worn Jim looked when one of them came up with the idea to put makeup on him while he slept. This idea was adapted unanimously. Like little mice they crept quietly into the back bedroom. Jim was deep asleep, and Mom knew that when he was this tired, it would take an earthquake to wake him. So the pack of she-wolves surrounded the bed and planned their attack. They darkened his eyebrows, and on his lips they put what looked to be half a tube of lipstick that ran off his lips, under his nose, and down near his jaw. They put nail polish on his fingers and toes. Like that wasn't enough, Clara came up with the idea to tie a bow around his penis. Mom ran to get ribbon, and she came back with a bright red ribbon, the kind used for gift-wrapping. Aunt Francis's face was beat red, and she said, "This is awful. I can't be a part of this," and with a suppressed giggle, she put her hands over her face and peeked through her fingers.

Now they had tied a huge bow on Jim's penis, and the job was done. He had eyebrow pencil, nail polish on his fingers and toes, and a mouth smeared in lipstick. Could you imagine if he woke up, had a heart attack, and was rushed to the ER? Imagine trying to explain this to the doctors and nurses on duty. But knowing Jim, I'm sure he would have thought of something.

Now the job was done, and the girls retired to the kitchen for tea and cookies. Mom actually thought this was a work of art. The girls were laughing and complimenting each other. About a half hour went by, and we heard Jim get up and walk into the bathroom. Still groggy, he looked into the medicine cabinet and was about to take a pee, with his hand on his ribbon-laden penis, when he looked at his made-up face and yelled from the bathroom, "I don't know what contest I entered, but I think I won first prize!" The girls roared with laughter. Then Jim said, "As soon as I'm done taking a piss, I'm gonna get even." With that the girls grabbed their coats and hats—Mom too—and ran for the front door. Jim heard them leaving and said, "You whores are nuts. You should be put away," and then he turned around and went back to bed and slept until noon the next day.

Doubles Buys
Thanksgiving Dinner

While Jim was still living at the house on Evans Street, on the day before Thanksgiving, Jim had guests staying at the house for the holiday: old friends Walter Tyski and his wife Joann. Everyone called Walter by his alias, Doubles, even his wife Joann. These people were quite unique. Walter traveled with the carnival named Straight Shows as a barker on the midway. He was also a champion booster (shoplifter). Joann was a madam who ran a cathouse in Buck's county. Doubles got his nickname back when he was a boy; he had a very large head for his body, and the kids called him Double Head. Over the years it was cut short to Doubles.

Now with Thanksgiving coming up and Doubles being a great booster, he volunteered to go shoplifting for Thanksgiving. We expected about thirty people between adults and kids. So my sister Pat, Jim, Doubles, and I were off to the supermarket. Jim was driving, and we stopped at a light and were in the turning lane to make a left into the shopping center where the market was located. While stopped at the light, Jim and Doubles were planning their assault on the store. Then the light turned green, and we got the arrow to make our left. We were the second car at the light, and the car ahead of us rounded the corner and made the left. As we approached the corner, a woman with her head down stepped right in front of our car, oblivious to time and space. Jim was on the ball and stopped the car on a dime. The woman was startled and just stood in front of the car; like a deer in headlights, she froze. Jim waited a bit, but the woman didn't move one way or the other. Then Jim rolled down his window, leaned out, and said "Hey, lady, let's go. Move it or get a snatch full of bumper." Another original gem had rolled off the lips of the old man—what poetry! The woman stepped back onto the sidewalk, and Jim made his left and said while passing, "Thanks, dear." Into the lot we went.

We parked near the front of the food market. Jim said, "Wait here," and Pat and I sat in the car while Jim and Doubles went in to do their boosting. About ten minutes later, they came back to the car empty-handed, not carrying any packages. Doubles was wearing a large coat that he referred to as his "shopping cart." This coat had several inside pockets, a hollowed-out lining, and outside pockets that were large vertical slits. You could put your hand into one vertical slit, and you would be inside the lining, and then there was another slit directly across, and when you put your hand through it, you were inside the coat where all the pockets were located. In other words, the slit on the outside was directly in line with the slit on the inside. It was like having a hole right through the coat.

Doubles would approach the shelves where items were placed, and his coat would be open, and he would lean against items on the shelves or over items in a display case. With his right hand in his pocket and through his coat, it was hidden from sight. So when he leaned over or against an item, the right hand was doing the lifting. Then he had the option to put the item in the pockets that were on the inside or to pull it into the inside lining because the coat was hollowed out. When he was going to take an item off a shelf, he would lean over it, covering it with his coat. He would use his left hand to take another item off the shelf and look at it. While he was doing this, the right hand was doing the lifting and putting the items inside his coat. The left hand was just for misdirection; he would make like he was reading a label or an ingredient and then place that item back onto the shelf. Meanwhile, the right hand had cleared everything below it.

Before Doubles got into the car, he unloaded the shopping cart. The volume of food that was extracted from the coat was unbelievable. All the inside pockets were full, as was the inside lining, and when he had finished unloaded it, the trunk of the car was almost full. He had enough food to feed thirty people. The only thing he didn't have was turkeys. Dad said he had a shitload of them in his freezer. (Gee, I wonder where he got them.) Now they were off to a liquor store in New Jersey that had an extensive list of fine wine. It was a short drive, maybe fifteen minutes, and we pulled up outside the liquor store. We were all going in, and Dad said to stick close to him when we got in the store and let Doubles go on his own. So as we entered the store, we walked toward the cheap wine, and Doubles headed for the fine wine.

As we pretended to browse, we were looking out the corner of our eyes trying to catch the champ in action. We didn't see a thing, and we even knew what he was doing. Maybe ten minutes went by, and Doubles smiled at Jim, and we all walked up to the checkout counter, but no one had anything in their hands. We walked right past the clerk at the counter and said, "Nice selection you have here." This put a smile on the clerk's face.

He replied, "We try."

Jim said, "We'll be back," and we all walked out.

What balls—we didn't buy a thing. When we got back to the car, Doubles gently took off his "shopping cart" (his coat) and handed it to Pat and me in the backseat. Doubles complimented Jim on his choice and said, "They have an excellent selection of fine wines and liquors, and from now on they get all my business!" When we got home, we took the booty into the kitchen, and Doubles unloaded his coat. He had a dozen bottles of fine red and white wine and one bottle of cognac (top-shelf) that he snagged for himself and another guest who would be sharing the holiday, Joe the Jew. Pat and I looked at each other in amazement; we hadn't seen him take a thing.

Thanksgiving Dinner Surprise

Now there was nothing to do but prepare the food for the next day. Mom had taken the turkeys out of the freezers, and they were already defrosting. We had two large turkeys, and Mom had two ovens and all the help she needed. Some of the people there were my brother Jim, his wife Lynn, my sister Pat and her daughters Diane and Robin, and my brothers Tony and Gerry and their guest, Peter Rabbit, a world-class pool hustler whose real name was Peter Linhard. Peter was a Jew who had escaped Germany when he was eleven years old, and he had some blood-curdling stories that he shared with just a few who were close to him.

Peter liked to talk and sing with an Irish brogue. Joe, aka Joe the Jew, and his wife Ida liked to talk and tell jokes with a Chinese accent, my uncle Barney and my aunt Patty were professional entertainers, and Barney was a stand-up comic who sang, danced, did impersonations, and told jokes. Patty was a singer and very good at it. She looked and sounded like Keely Smith, a big star of the 1940s and 1950s. We thought she sang better than Keely. And my uncle Frank was loud and always spoke at a shout, and his wife Girt always spoke at a whisper. She was always telling Frank to shut his loud mouth. Next, was my Aunt Clara who was my mother's best friend and a great person. She liked to curse a little—well a lot. And my sister brought a guest, Anna, whom she'd known for only a few weeks. Anna was a unique creature. She had the appearance of a voodoo doll. With ours not being a judgmental group, she went unnoticed for a while.

When dinner was ready, it looked like a feast for royalty. While the women were dishing the food out and bringing it from the kitchen, Joann was telling the girls of her exploits at the whorehouse. This had them laughing while they worked. Once the food was out and everyone was seated, the seating was worked this way: There were three large tables, one in the dining room, one in the living room, and one in the den. The senior adults were in the dining room, the next generation in the living room, and the next generation in the den. The floor plan of the house was laid out in a circle. As you walked in the front door, you were in the living room, and as you walked to your right and then to your left, you were in the dining room. As you walked through the dining room, you were in the kitchen. As you walked through the kitchen, you turned left and walked into the den. As you walked through the den and turned left you were back in the living room. There was a large arch between the dining room and the living room, and both rooms had fireplaces. And all the rooms were separated by a stairway that was almost in the center of the house and that led to the second floor. So the grownups in the living room and dining room could see one another and converse, and the kids in the den could be heard but not seen.

Now it was time to dig in. Everyone remarked how beautiful the silverware and the crystal were. Jim said, "It should be; it came out of the finest houses. Nothing but the best for you assholes." My brother Jim, my uncle Barney, and my dad had the largest appetites, and they were ready to start eating when Pat said her friend Anna wanted to say a prayer of thanks.

Uncle Barney let out a slight moan, and Uncle Frank whispered to Barney, "You can wait another minute before you eat, you fuckin' heathen." This brought muffled laughter from our end of the table. Then Anna lifted the palms of her hands over her head, pointed at the ceiling, and then lowered her head almost onto her plate and started to chant and howl and wail and sway around in her chair from side to side. Uncle Frank, while looking at Anna and talking out the side of his mouth toward the other end of the table, loudly whispered, "What the fuck is this?" Everyone was trying not to laugh. I had a dog at the time, a female Samoyed named Russia. Russia was sitting behind me on the floor, and as Anna moaned and howled, Russia moaned and howled. It became a howling match. Anna wasn't bothered in the least that the animal was barking and howling. Everyone was doing their best not to laugh out loud.

I couldn't take it anymore and got up from the table and went into the upstairs bathroom. I put a towel over my mouth, trying not to make any noise. I was laughing so hard I saw stars. Seconds later, I was joined in the bathroom by what seemed to be half the guests who had also lost it. When the howling subsided, we pulled ourselves together and threw water on our faces. Now we were refreshed and ready to join the brave souls that had sat through the howling. We were once again seated and beginning to pass dishes of food. There were still whispers and suppressed laughter, but Anna wasn't done making her mark. She was eating with her hands, picking up food with her fingers. She had filling under her nails and on the sides of her mouth and cheeks. My brother Jim, a Vietnam vet who thought he'd seen it all, was staring at her in disbelief. Anna, who only minutes ago had made everyone laugh, now was making everyone's stomach turn.

My brother Tony asked politely, "Why do you eat with your hands?"

Anna replied, "Knives and forks are the devil's tools." God wanted her to be natural and use the hands he gave her. There would be no more questions; she was obviously the craziest one of the bunch (and that's saying something). My brother Jim, Lynn, Gerry, Charlie (Sabu), and I had lost our appetites. Those with stronger stomachs were doing well. Anna requested the little tail that hung off the turkey's butt. She was now munching on the turkey's butt. Then the pièce de résistance—Anna started to sneeze and cough, and with her hands covered with food, she did not cover her nose and mouth with a napkin, but leaned her head back and was looking straight up at the ceiling. She let go a sneeze that shot a vapor of bodily fluids up and cascading down onto the dinner table, landing on food and guests alike. This stopped the remaining diners. My sister Pat had outdone herself. Pat was known to have some quirky friends, but Anna was the showstopper. Luckily, Anna finished eating, coughing, sneezing, and howling and said she had to go home before the sun went down (sounding like a confused vampire).

Everyone responded, a little tongue in cheek, with things like, "Ahh, you gotta go soon?" And Uncle Frank whispered to my sister, "What's she gonna do next, shit on the floor?" Anna, smiling at everyone, got up from the table and said she loved everyone and was going to pray for us. The crowd grinned with half-smiles, hoping she didn't mean now. Pat had driven her to the house and had to take her home and said she'd be right back because Anna didn't live far. After they left, the place buzzed with conversation, and we figured we could salvage dessert. We had something to talk about over coffee and cake, and we could try to erase the images of the day.

When Pat got back, Jim said, "If you ever bring anything into the house that even looks like that again, you'll be disowned."

Pat replied, "Oh, don't bother to thank me now. Wait till you hear this."

Mom said, "There's more?" Pat said that Anna had tried to kiss her in the car on the way home and had said she wanted to make love to her. After seeing how Anna dined, this conjured up an image in my mind that I've been unable to get rid of for thirty-five years.

Serge the Attack Dog Breaks Free

Jim and Mary had a friend named Bud Walling. Like Jim and Mary, he was in the horse business. Bud lived just outside of Philadelphia on a large estate on the Delaware River. Bud's wife name is Sesly. How they met is quite interesting. Bud was on vacation in Florida and going to the racetrack everyday in Hialeah, and that's where he met Sesly. She had been accompanying a Russian dignitary, a man of wealth and power. Although she was living with this man, she was not married to him. She had been taken from her village when she was thirteen. She was now twenty-two and very unhappy. Over a period of days at the track talking to each other, Bud and Sesly became attracted. As the story goes, Sesly got up to go to the lady's room at the track, left with Bud, and never came back.

Whether Bud and Sesly ever got married, no one knew, but they were happy, and at the time of this story, they had been together for over ten years. During the Second World War, Bud was in the army, and he trained attack dogs. Years after his release from the army, he was living up on the river, where he had lots of ground and thought he could use a guard dog, so he purchased a German shepherd and trained him to be a guard/attack dog. When not given any commands around people, he was playful and docile.

Jim and Mary had spent plenty of time at Bud's estate and knew the dog well. The dogs name was Sergeant. One day in late spring or early summer Bud came to visit, and he brought Sesly and Sergeant along. We also lived in a large estate on Roosevelt Boulevard with plenty of ground and trees. As Bud pulled up our driveway and stopped at the house, he and Sesly got out of the car, and Bud reached in the back and pulled out Sergeant, who was on a choker collar and a long leather leash. Bud took the dog to a shady tree and tied him to it. Mom brought the dog water, and Serge was content to lay in the cool shade. After a couple of hours, Jim and Bud were talking in the kitchen in the back of the house, and Sesly and Mom were sitting on the porch in front of the house near where Serge was tied.

We had a dog of our own at the time, and his name was Terry. He was a small fox terrier and no match for Serge, so he was kept inside the house. But somehow Terry got out and ran directly over to where Serge was tied and began barking

111

and taunting Serge. I guess he figured, "Who's this big lug on my lawn?" Serge immediately rose to his feet, rolling his lip and showing his teeth, trying to get at Terry. Terry, staying just out of range, was doing an excellent job of pissing him off. Then Terry's luck ran out. Serge broke free and started to chase Terry toward the house. Terry got up on the porch toward the front door but didn't make it. Serge pounced down on him and slammed his jaws shut around the little dog's entire midsection and began shaking him like a rag. The sounds of the growling and barking and my mother's bloodcurdling screams reached all the way into the kitchen, where my father sat with Bud. Jim thought the dog had attacked my mother, and he tore through the house and out the front door and onto the front porch. Without hesitation, he grabbed Serge by his throat with one hand, lifting him off the ground, and punched the dog in the head, knocking him unconscious.

Serge was lying on the porch like he was dead. Terry was also lying on the porch; his guts had been ripped out, but he was still alive. Everyone was hysterical. Jim got a blanket and wrapped Terry in it, trying to pick up his stomach at the same time. Jim and I rushed the dog to the vet. On the way, Jim said "He's not gonna make it." We went into the veterinarian's operating room.

The vet took one look at the animal and said, "This animal's talkin' to the angels. What do you want me to do?"

Jim said, "What can you do?"

The vet replied, "I can try to put everything back, but I can't promise you anything."

Jim said, "I don't care what it costs. Please try." And we left Terry in the hands of the doctor.

When we got home, we told Mom what the vet had said. She said she was going to pray for her companion. At about seven the next morning, the phone rang, and it was the vet himself. We were anticipating bad news. He said, "Terry made it through the night and was drinking water. Although this was remarkable, I can't promise you anything." Well the vet didn't even expect him to make it through the operation, but the pooch was still with us.

A few days later, the vet called and said, "Come get him. He'll be better off convalescing at home." And soon after, he was back on his feet, running and playing as if nothing had happened. Yet we noticed that when we opened the door to let him out, he looked like a cautious pedestrian crossing a busy street. He looked both ways before taking a step. Mom said that her prayers were answered. Jim said the dog had balls. Whatever it was, we were happy with the result. (P.S. Serge recovered from the punch, but now before leaving the house, he looks both ways for Jim.)

Trailer Load of Color TVs

One day, at about 9 AM, the phone rang at Jim's house. He picked it up, and it was Whitey Checki. Whitey worked for a trucking company as a dispatcher and yard jockey. His job was to dispatch the trucks and jockey them around the yard so as to put them in order in rows, with the first to leave in the front row and so on. The cargoes were diverse, everything from coffee and nuts to bolts and lumber. Whitey kept track of everything that came in and out of the yard. This time he had a trailer load of color TVs, but he had a problem. He wanted to steal them but didn't know how to do it without getting caught, so he called Jim to tell him his problem. Jim listened to what he had to say and then asked, "How long will they be in the yard?"

Whitey said, "Two days."

Jim said, "No problem. We're gonna make some money, and I'm gonna cover your ass." Now Whitey's son, Bluff, worked at the yard in the same capacity as Whitey. He worked from 8 AM to 4 PM, and Whitey worked from 4 PM to twelve midnight. This meant that if the truck was taken at 8 AM, no one would know it was missing till after midnight, when the watchman came on duty. Jim told Whitey he had sixteen hours to work, and they didn't need to steal the truck of TVs, just borrow it for a few hours. He explained to Whitey what he had planned and Whitey's part in it. They were going to sell the truckload of TVs, but not steal them, and he already had a buyer in mind, a guy who was hanging around the poolroom (the Moulin Rouge) who liked to bet on pool games and flash large sums of money and who claimed he had received a large settlement from a divorce with a rich wife. If he wasn't bullshitting, his bundle was about to be downsized.

Jim hung up the phone and headed for the poolroom. As you walked through the front door of the poolroom, to your right was a large sitting area with a TV and magazines where people waited for pool tables to become available during busy times and where pool hustlers congregated to scheme and make games. When Jim walked through the door, the guy that he told Whitey about was sitting on one of the sofas watching the TV. Now time was of the essence, so Jim walked over, sat down, and started talking to the mark. The guys name was Al.

They talked for about fifteen minutes, and then the door to the poolroom opened and a fellow walked in, looked around, and looking over toward Jim and Al, said, "Do you know where I could find Jimmy D'Angelo?"

Jim said, "Yeah, I'm Jimmy D'Angelo. What can I do for you?"

The guy replied, "I have something that might interest you." Jim got up from where he was sitting and walked over to a cigarette machine and motioned for the guy to come over. They were now about ten feet or so from Al, and they were talking just loud enough that Al could catch every other word, or at least the ones that counted ("make some money," "hot color TVs," and so on), just enough to put the hook in Al. In a few minutes the guy said loudly, "OK, I'll be back in about an hour." (By the way, the mystery man was Whitey Checki.)

Whitey had no sooner walked out the door when Al said, "I couldn't help overhearing that guy wants to sell a truckload of TVs."

Jim looked at Al suspiciously before answering (he was playing hard to get), and after a short pause he said, "Yeah, yeah, he wants to move them right away, and I could turn them over in a day. I could have them drop them at my shop." (Jim had a warehouse where he did his furniture work.) Then Jim explained that he had a guy who would buy the whole load, and forty thousand in profit could be made on the deal, but the guy selling them wanted cash when he dropped them off, and the load would cost forty thousand. Jim could make forty thousand the following day because his buyer would pay eighty, but Jim said he only had twenty thousand of his own, though he was sure he could make some calls and get the other twenty.

Al knew that Jim was constantly making deals out of the poolroom. Al was gnawing at the bit. He took the bait and said he could come up with the other twenty, and he and Jim would be fifty-fifty partners.

Jim replied, "You know this is illegal, but its low-risk and a high return on the money. You better think about it. I'm going to make some calls."

Al pleaded, "No, I don't care if it's illegal. I can get my end in less than a half hour."

What could Jim do? After all, he did ask nicely. Jim said, "OK, I have to go get mine. I'll meet you back here in half an hour or so." So Al went to the bank to get his money, and Jim went home (he kept that much cash at the house). He also wanted to have lunch with Whitey and explain the rest of the scam. After they had a bite and a talk, Whitey went to get the truck, and Jim went back to the poolroom to meet Al. When Jim walked in, Al was already there. Jim had his money in a brown paper bag that he was carrying under his arm. He had Al put his twenty thousand in the bag, and Jim stashed it back under his arm. A few minutes went by before Whitey came back into the poolroom. He looked at Jim, and Jim waved him over to sit with him and Al.

Whitey sat down and said to Jim, "Can I talk to you alone?"

Jim said, "It's OK. He's my partner. We got the cash and we're ready to go. Let me give you directions to the drop-off." Then he wrote out directions as if Whitey had never been to Jim's shop. This was to give the impression that they were not familiar with one another. In reality, Whitey was at the shop almost as much as Jim. Now it was off to the shop. Jim said to Al, "Let's take your car."

Al was excited and visibly nervous. He did not have nerves of steel or nerves to steal, but eagerly said "OK." Jim directed him to the shop. Jim's shop ran from street to street, so when they pulled up, they were in the back of the shop. They got out of the car and walked up a short dead-end alleyway. At the end of the alleyway, there were two doors, one on the left and one on the right. The one on the left was a side entrance to Jim's shop. The one on the right went into a neighboring building. When they entered Jim's shop, they were in his office. In the front of the office, there were glass windows and a glass door with blinds slightly opened and slanted downward, so that you could see movement out in the warehouse, but your view was somewhat obstructed.

Jim put the bag of money on the desk in the office and went out in the warehouse where he opened a huge sliding door that had wheels on the base of it and counterbalances of steel weights to allow one strong person to open it. After opening the door, he walked back into his office, closing the door behind him, and sat at his desk with Al and told him all the arrangements were made to have everything picked up early the next afternoon, and they would have their cash. They would make twenty thousand profit a piece. Just then, the back end of a truck appeared at the doors and stopped. Whitey got out of the truck and walked into the shop and asked Jim and Al to guide him back and tell him where to stop. The truck was too long to back all the way in, so about half of it was in the shop and half of it was out in the street. Whitey got out of the truck this time with a helper, but before they were going to unload, they wanted to see the cash. Jim said, "Sure," and invited them into the office.

Whitey came in without the helper, and Jim, Al, and Whitey counted the money at the desk. When they were done, Jim put it all back in the bag. Al and Jim sat in the office while Whitey and his helper started to unload the truck. Jim was sitting with the money in his lap and talking to Al when a disturbance of loud voices and shouting came from the shop. Jim jumped up and ran to the door, with the bag of money in his hand, and opened the door just in time to hear a loud voice say, "Get the fuck out here! Put your hands on your head. You're under arrest."

Jim looked over his shoulder back in the office, mouthed the word "run" to Al, and quickly motioned with his head toward the back door. Then, walking out into the warehouse, he shut the office door behind him and, a loud voice said, "Up against the fuckin wall!"

Then a second loud voice said, "Check in the office," creating just enough time, hopefully, for Al to make his getaway out the back door and down the alley to his car. The so-called cop (one of the players) went into the office and Al was gone. Then he announced loudly, "There's a back door," in case Al had just run back to the alley and stopped. When the guy opened the door and looked down the alley, like Houdini, Al had disappeared. Now Jim, Whitey, his helper, and the two bogus cops reloaded the truck, and Whitey had it back in the yard before his shift started. The so-called cops were two mob-connected strong-armed guys from south Jersey who had worked with Jim on many other hustles. The kid with Whitey was a neighbor from Port Richmond.

Jim had received the call from Whitey at about 9 AM in the morning, and by 2 PM, the money was in their hands, and no one was the wiser. Al had seen Jim around the poolroom many times before this, but he only knew Jim as a hustler and did not know his home phone or where he lived. So to make contact, he would have to go back to the poolroom, and that's where he had met the guy who stole the TVs. He did not want to take the chance of possibly being "fingered" and arrested. So Al didn't return to the poolroom for almost a year, and Jim told Al that the truck driver had given a description of him to the cops. Jim said that he hadn't said anything and that it had cost him a bundle to get an expensive lawyer, and now he was on probation. Jim said, "Although you and I were partners, fifty-fifty, I don't expect you to pay half of my lawyers' expenses, but if you want to kick in a little, it wouldn't hurt." Now with his life of crime behind him, Al left the poolroom, never to be seen again.

The Parlor Game of Family Opinions

One evening, the family was gathered around the dining room table at the house on Evans Street. There was Mom, Pat, Charlie (Pat's husband), Peggy Hartley (our neighbor), my brothers Jim, Gerri and Tony, my wife Kelly, and me (Bernie). Jimmy D was sitting at the kitchen table about ten feet away. The dining room and the kitchen were in plain view of each other. Jim was quietly reading his Bible, the *Morning Telegraph* (a horse racing paper). He was totally submerged and studying hard to pick a winner to bet on at the next day's racing at Liberty Bell Park (a racetrack about ten minutes from the house).

At the same time, in the dining room, chitchat and small talk were center stage when Pat came up with an idea. She said, "Let's all talk about ourselves, giving a description of our personalities and how we think people see us." Before anyone could answer, yeah or nah, Pat started to give her description of herself. She said, "I'm artistic, intelligent, witty, pretty, and easy to get along with." It seemed Pat thought highly of herself. This opened the door for comments. Charlie, Pat's husband, jumped on the statement Pat had made about being easy to get along with. He laughingly said that if she was easy to get along with, he couldn't imagine what difficult would be. This did not sit well with Pat. Now the insults were flying. Charlie should have kept his big mouth shut. When it was his turn to talk about himself, he should have added stupid to his résumé. This game was going to be fun. It took about five minutes for Pat to stop screaming and hurling insults at Charlie. She finally settled down to just intermittent insults and an occasional threat. Gee, do you think that Pat might not be as easy to get along with as she claimed?

Well, this set the standard for the evening. We each took a turn giving descriptions of ourselves and how we thought people saw us. The self-praise ran rampant. Everyone thought that they were wonderful, and as each of us took our turn building ourselves up, the others took great pleasure in knocking us down to reality. There were no holds barred. We each thought we were wonderful and were prepared to argue the point. Not one person gave a description of themselves that was unanimously accepted. Meanwhile, in the kitchen Jim had his head buried in the racing form and never uttered a word. He just kept studying. It must have taken a couple of hours for everyone to be heard. We were out of people to criticize.

My mother looked into the kitchen and said to Jim, "How do you think people see you?" Without lifting his head or taking his eyes off the racing sheet he roared, "Me, I'm a motherfucker!" and continued to study his racing form. Jim had just done in one small sentence what everyone else couldn't do in several hours. For the first time all evening, there wasn't a rebuttal, just laughter. In a house full of self-praise—and it's said that self-praise stinks—Jim came out smelling like rose.

Jim Needs Transfusions to Stay Alive

Jim's shop, where he pulled off the TV caper, was located in a tough neighborhood. It was tough in the respect that teenage kids would break into the garages and the warehouses to steal whatever they thought they could use or sell. In the section of Philadelphia where Jim's shop was located, it was not unusual to have one street with houses and the next street with garages, warehouses, and body and fender shops and so on. Jim had a large commercial-size garage about forty feet wide and about fifty feet deep with a high ceiling. Jim had an eye for picking out gang leaders. He would warm up to them and get them to work delivering furniture, and he paid them well. He charmed them—after all, he was a lot like them, just older. He showed them respect, and friendships were formed. He also paid them to watch his place so that no one would break in and vandalize. These kids did not know the value of the furniture that was in the shop. So Jim had the vandals and thieves watching over his shop. It was better than the best burglar alarm and protection money could buy. Almost all of the other shops were broken into, some more than once, but Jim's went untouched.

Over the years of working in the shop, spraying lacquers and thinners and other finishers and solvents, Jim acquired a blood problem He was sick for about five years, but the only one who knew how sick was my mother. It became apparent when Jim lost weight and weakened. He was rapidly losing strength and could barely sit up and walk. He was getting blood transfusions to stay alive. He needed an operation to have his spleen removed, but no doctor would touch him because they said he was too sick and weak to survive an operation. Jim's nephew, a lawyer from Miami, heard of the problem from my mother. A few days later, he called back to talk to Jim and said that he had two guys who were willing to look at him. This was more than what was happening locally. Jim was in terrible pain and had been for a year and now was days away from death, but he was still optimistic and had yet to complain. Jim's nephew, Francis Sevier, whom Jim had helped with his education, was now paying Jim back. His timing was perfect.

With not a minute to lose, Jim and I jumped on a plane and headed to Miami. Jim was in a wheelchair, unable to walk. I took him to Miami hospital where he saw a surgeon, Bob Zappa. After a short interview Dr. Zappa said he did not know if Jim, in his weakened condition, could stand the operation. Jim, just able to lift his head, said, "I survived forty-five years with my old lady—you ain't gonna kill me!" Dr. Zappa smiled and said that if and only if the hematologist agreed, he would do the job. Jim lit up like a Christmas tree, and we were off to another part of the hospital to see the hematologist, who already had Jim's records. His name was Dr. Harrington. When we got to talk to him, with Dr. Zappa present, he also said he didn't think Jim could survive. Dr. Harrington turned to Zappa and was discussing what he needed to do to Jim's blood to build him up. He was shaking his head from side to side. It did not look encouraging.

Then Jim spoke up and said, "If you do nothing, I'm gonna die anyway, so fuck it. Let's give it our best shot, and to make sure you guys give it your best shot, I'm not paying you until the job's done."

The doctors turned to each other and laughed and whispered to each other, and then Harrington turned around and said, "You're on!" The stage was set, and it was out of my hands. I had to leave my father there, not knowing if he was strong enough to make it through the night. Would this be the last time I would see him? I went to my cousin Frank's house and told him the news. He called my mother and told her to come down to Miami because Jim was going to be operated on, and she arrived the next afternoon. She was picked up by Francis's wife Natalie and was brought back to the house before going to the hospital. They were still beefing Jim up for the operation, and we couldn't see him till late in the day. Mom and I talked on the way to the hospital. She was preparing herself to let him go. After what the doctors had had to say, she didn't think he would live.

When we got to the hospital, Jim was in great spirits. You wouldn't think he was fighting for his life. We didn't talk much because he was very weak and needed all the strength he could muster. Nurses and orderlies were preparing to take him to the operating room. We kissed him goodbye and left him smiling as we walked out of the room. I looked back, and he winked. I thought that that would be the last time I would see my old man alive. The notion that "big boys don't cry" is bullshit. We stayed several hours till the operation was over. We were told that he was in intensive care and doing well. They didn't know how long he would be there, but they said he was sleeping and would be for hours. So we curled up on the furniture in the waiting room and pretended to sleep. A few hours went by and then a nurse came in and told us he was being moved to his room. He was still alive—this in itself was a small miracle.

When we got to his room, he was still sleeping. It was late, and the nurse told us that we should get some rest and come back later. My mother went home with Natalie, and I told her I would call if he woke. I stayed in the room the rest of the night. During the night I fell asleep. The next morning, I awoke, and Jim was sitting in a chair next to his bed with an intravenous feed in his arm. He looked at me with a broken smile. The tough old bastard was still breathing. I was ecstatic! He said, just barely holding his head up (he looked awful), "I feel fuckin' terrible, really rough," and he rolled his eyes, lowering his chin on his chest. I got up and sat on the windowsill in his room. I told him I was going to Francis and Natalie's to pick up Mom and bring her to see him. He again raised his head slowly and said, "Let her stay at Francis's for a while—I feel fuckin awful." Then he continued, "Don't hang around. Go into Miami, enjoy yourself, get laid," and he let out a weak laugh. "Come back tomorrow; I'll feel better. I need time to get on my feet." Two days ago he was dying, and now he needs a day to get back on his feet!

Just then Drs. Zappa and Harrington came into the room. They were astonished that he was sitting in a chair. Dr. Harrington asked, "How did you get there?"

Jim answered, "I got there myself."

The doctors looked at each other and shook their heads and said to Jim, "Now you gotta pay us."

With his head hanging on his chest, he once again looked up with half a smile and said, "Take a check?" Knowing Jim's background, they both let out a laugh. Jim was already trying to make people laugh.

Dr. Zappa added, "Jim, you're a miracle."

Jim in his weak voice said, "Yeah, it's a fuckin' miracle you guys didn't kill me." This started the doctors laughing again. Then Jim gently said, "Thanks." It was the opinion of the doctors that he had cheated death. How poetic—Jim even cheated the grim reaper. Before we knew it, Jim was out of the hospital and was on a plane and back in Philly doing business after being housebound for a couple of weeks.

Convalescing Pays Off

While Jim was convalescing, he came up with the idea to work at home. He decided to rob his own house. He was determined to make his downtime pay off. So Jim called Joe the Jew, the jeweler, and got jewelry appraisals on jewelry he didn't own. Then Jim called his insurance agent and got special coverage on forty thousand dollars' worth of imaginary jewelry. The adjustor, being a member of the family, was eager to oblige. This was in the middle of the summer. Jim planned to do a bit of house cleaning around January, and this would take care of Christmas bills. Now there was only one problem: my mother would never go for it. So Jim offered to send my mother to Florida to visit Francis and Natalie in late January. It would be a break from the frigid weather. Mom jumped at the chance. This also was the ideal time to do this because early evening in the winter, the neighbors would be eating dinner or watching TV, and with all the distractions inside the home, they would not be paying much attention to what's outside. So Jim could break into his house without anyone being the wiser, and to make sure Mom did not renege on her trip, Dad said he would also send her best girlfriend, my aunt Clara, and pay all the expenses. Although it would cost him a couple of bucks to add Clara, he said it gave the deal reassurance and sometimes "you gotta spend money to make money." What a businessman.

Soon January rolled around, and Mom was off to Florida, and Dad was left to ransack the house. Jim just simply locked up the house. The back door that led into our kitchen had six small panes of glass. Jim simply broke the one nearest the locks, put his hand in, and opened the door. No 007 here. Knowing how burglars ransack and root, Jim took only about five minutes to complete his job. Then he went over to the poolroom for the rest of the evening. He left the house around 7 PM and was back about 10 PM. He drove up his driveway, pretended to discover the break-in, called the police, and then went to the next-door neighbors' house and told them what had happened. The neighbors walked back to Jim's house with him, saying they didn't see or hear anything. The police pulled up. They went into the house, looked around, and had Jim looking with them. Jim had a small safe in the closet of his bedroom. The safe was gone. He told the police of the jewelry that was kept there. Jim had a list memorized of the jewelry and a few other items that he gave to the police. Without much questioning, the police were gone.

The only thing left to do was call the claim into the insurance company. The agent I spoke of earlier was an immediate member of the family. He had a direct number to his desk and a predetermined time to call. When Jim got the agent on the phone, he told the agent of the burglary. The agent then said, "Do you mind if I tape this call for my records?"

Jim replied, "No, not at all," and he started to tell him of his misfortune. He started to cry and sob on the phone saying, "My poor wife's gonna be a nervous wreck. She's gonna come home from vacation and find her home has been violated. She'll never feel safe again. Oh my God this is awful!"

The agent, comforting Jim, said, "We'll do our best, Mr. D'Angelo, to help you."

I was sitting next to my dad when he made this call, and he had me believing him. He did a masterful job of portraying a victim. Jim never told the neighbors or anyone about the claim for the jewelry and other items. He just said that the thieves had wrecked the place and didn't get anything. So when Mom came home from Florida, she wouldn't think Jim had anything to do with it. Mom and Clara came back from Florida two weeks later, and by then, things had quieted down. The house was all cleaned up and put back together, and the burglary was attributed to kids, said my father, but just the same, he was going to get an alarm.

The adjustor called Jim to tell him he had his check, and he was going to bring it to him, but there were a few things that Jim and Mom needed to sign. This was no problem because Jim signed Mom's name as good as he signed his own. Now the adjuster would get his cut, and Joe the Jeweler would get his cut. Jim took 60 percent, and Joe and the adjuster split forty after expenses were taken off the top. Now that this plan had worked, Jim was lining up people to play victims. At the top of the list was anyone who owed him money, and down the list was anyone who needed money. Of course, Jim got a large chunk of all the settlements. This was an add-on to Jim's whiplash business. He had the lawyers, who had the doctors. He had the adjustors, who had the collision experts (body and fender shops). One summer, it looked like half of northeast Philadelphia was wearing neck braces. Jim was doing this long before it was common. Before the general public caught on, Jim was on to new horizons.

PART IV

Tallahassee Comes to Philadelphia

One summer, Jim imported out-of-town pool hustlers into Philadelphia, and without telling Mom, he kept the first guy at our house. This guy's name—or what he went by—was Tallahassee. As soon as Tallahassee came into town, Jim took him out all night pool hustling. Now after a night of hustling, Jim and Tallahassee wandered home about noon, never informing Mom that she had a houseguest. Mom wasn't home when they came in, and Dad told Tallahassee to go sleep in my and my brother Jim's room, where there were two twin beds. He could take his pick of the two. The weary pool shooter stripped down to his jockey shorts and proceeded to lie down spread eagle and fall fast asleep.

Tallahassee had an ominous presence. He was a six-foot-six, three-hundred-pound black man, so when he hit the sheets on a single bed, he covered every square inch of it. Jim went into his own room and in no time was cutting zees. So while the two bad boys slept, no one knew they were there. Meanwhile, Mom and my sister Pat were at a neighbor's house socializing, drinking tea, and chatting (or, according to Jim, "shooting the shit"). It was getting close to dinnertime, and Pat and Mom headed home. Once into the house, Mom went into the kitchen to start dinner, and Pat went upstairs to use the bathroom. When Pat got to the top of the steps, my bedroom was to her right, and the door was ajar, making visible the huge male form of Tallahassee clad only in jockey shorts and lying spread eagle. She turned right around and went down to the kitchen to report to Mom her find. Mom had a houseguest, and she hadn't been given prior notice. Someone had invaded the queen's castle, and Jim was in deep shit.

Now Mom stormed up the stairs, peaked in at Tallahassee, and then headed into Jim's room. Jim was fast asleep. She woke him up, and he opened his eyes to see a fire-eating dragon. Mom was pissed because she hadn't been told that she was going to have a houseguest, and her daughter had come upon a half-naked stranger. She asked, "Who's that in the other bedroom?"

Jim, in a twilight sleep, smiled and said, "That's Tallahassee, and he's a pooool-shootin motherfucker!" Jim was happy, so they must have had a good night's hustle (made money).

Mom, hearing this, said, "Don't ever bring anyone into this house to stay without talking to me first, or I'll throw you and your uninvited guests out on your asses." She said that she was going downstairs and dinner would be ready in one hour, and she expected to see Jim and that "pooool-shootin motherfucker" at the table on time. A little less than an hour later, Jim and his protégé came limping down the stairs to the kitchen to check out Mom's attitude. Upon entering the kitchen, Jim immediately introduced Tallahassee to Mom.

As big as Tallahassee was, he was nevertheless soft-spoken and mannerly. "How do you do, ma'am? It's my pleasure to meet you," he said with a soft southern drawl. Mom was gone with the wind; she had just been swooned by a twenty-five-year-old smooth-talking hustler. She pulled out a chair at the dinner table and told Tallahassee to sit. Seeing this, Jim looked over at me and smiled as if to say that the dragon had lost her fire. Jim didn't even get this treatment. Mom was in a place where women love to go; she had the yin and yang of life. She had a handsome young man to flatter her and show respect, and on the other hand, there was Jim, on whom she could whip up and get out her frustrations. Tallahassee was treated like a son. All was calm on the home front.

As we sat around the kitchen table, Tallahassee told of the night of fun and fortune he had had with Jim. Tallahassee worked with Jim for about another week or so, and then Jim brought another pool hustler to town, but this time was sure to tell Mom about the pending houseguest (another six-foot-plus, two-hundred-fifty-pound black guy who went by the name of Cherry Soda—that's right, Cherry Soda). He too was very well-mannered and swooned Mom and got the VIP treatment. Jim made a little money hustling with Cherry Soda, and then he was history. Next up was a pool player who called himself Allentown, and Jim made a couple bucks with him. Allentown was a short white guy: Jim was an equal opportunity employer. Allentown was also a charmer and he too got the A treatment.

Jersey Jerry Meets Peter Rabbit

Another of Jim's houseguests was a pool shooter named Jerry Hunt. Finally, someone with a real name. He wasn't named after a soft drink or city. We just called him Jerry. Jerry was tall and thin and looked like the country singer Alan Jackson. He was not only well-mannered, but also handsome. I thought Mom was going to keep this one and throw Jim out. Jim took Jerry every place he thought he could make a game. Jerry beat everyone in sight. Then the word got, out and no one would play Jerry. It was time to say goodbye, but Jim came up with an idea. Jerry would play another hustler, the best around: Peter Rabbit (Peter Linhard). This would bring in huge amounts of betting money and fill the Moulin Rouge poolroom to the doors. Jim took care of the details, and the game was on.

The players agreed to play a game known as "nine ball." They would play for the best out of ten games. Peter Rabbit was a two-to-one favorite to beat the newcomer. People came from all over to bet on the game, 90 percent of them were betting on the Rabbit to win, and Jim took all the action. He was Jerry's backer. Although Jim and Peter were lifelong friends, this was business. The stage was set for a Saturday at 5 PM. (By the way, someone asked Jerry where he was from, and Jerry said north Jersey. So guess what? Now Jerry was nicknamed after a state: everyone started calling him Jersey Jerry. We now had a state versus a cartoon character.)

Saturday rolled around, and the Moulin Rouge Poolroom was filled to capacity. If you've never played pool, it's not likely you'll know what nine ball is or how it's played. Here's an abridged explanation. Nine ball is played with nine balls numbered one through nine and a cue ball (no number and white in color). The cue ball is shot at the numbered balls in numerical order: number one first, then two, then three, and so on. To win you must sink the nine, and this is done by shooting it into one of six pockets in a pool table. The nine can also be sunk on the break, and that is an automatic win. The break is when the balls one through nine are gathered at the far end of the table and put into a device called a rack. This corrals the balls together. Then the cue ball is placed at the opposite end of the table, and a player uses what is known as a cue stick (a long dowel-like instrument) to drive the cue ball into the numbered balls at the far end of the table. Ideally the balls will be moved around in such a manner that one or more may drop into one of the six pockets on the table. If the nine should happen to go in, this is an immediate win. If not, the remaining balls must be shot in rotation till the nine is reached. Then a player must sink the nine ball in the pocket for the win.

One other shortcut may happen when during the shooting in rotation, any of the balls one through eight is shot into the nine and the nine is sunk. This is called a combination shot, and by sinking the nine, the player gains a win. Again, the only way to win is to sink the nine. A player can sink one through seven and miss the eight, and then his or her opponent would just have to sink the eight and nine to win. So you can sink the majority of balls and still lose. The object is the nine. It's an extremely difficult game by any standards, but expert players sometimes make it look easy.

Now game day rolled around, and the Moulin Rouge poolroom was packed to the doors with gamblers, onlookers, and awed amateurs. When the doors opened, in walked the two-to-one favorite and local boy, Peter Rabbit. A few minutes later, Jimmy D and Jersey Jerry made their entrance. You could feel the excitement. There hadn't been anything like this in a long time. The two combatants took their two-piece custom-made pool cues out of their leather carrying cases and started to assemble them. They agreed to flip a coin to see who would break (go first). Going first is an advantage. Jim simply flipped a coin into the air over the pool table. Peter chose heads and Jerry chose tails, and the coin came down to rest on the table. The coin showed tails, and Jersey Jerry won the break.

Players of this caliber have been known to make all the balls on the table several games in a row, with the opponent sometimes never even getting a shot. Tonight they were playing the best out of ten. This meant that the first man to win six games would take the money. The amount at stake on the table was ten thousand dollars. The gamblers and fans bet several times that amount on Peter Rabbit to win, and Jim booked all the action. In short, this meant that if Jersey Jerry lost, Jim would take a serious bath.

Now the balls were being racked for the first game, and silence filled the Moulin as handsome Jerry walked up to the table with his pearl-handled pool cue and prepared to break for the first game, and with a thunderous thrust of the cue, Jerry made three balls on the break, among them the nine. The first game was over in less than a heartbeat. The room was full of heavy breathing coming from shocked Peter Rabbit fans. The balls were racked and ready for the second game. Jerry approached the table and again with a thunderous smash sunk three balls.

This time the nine was still on the table. The one, the three, and the six were gone, so the first ball to be shot was the two, and it was in line with the nine. It could be made in the left corner pocket. Jerry shot the combination, and game two was over. Now you could hear a pin drop. Jerry had won two games in a row, and the balls were being racked for a third game. The silence was deafening, but then it was broken by the sound of Peter's voice.

Peter said to Jerry, "What religion are you?"

Jerry replied, "Methodist. Why?"

Peter replied, "I got to make a change."

Jerry replied, "Why?"

Peter answered, "Are you kidding right now? It's Methodists two, Jews zero."

This broke the ice and got a huge laugh from the fans. Now it was back to business. Jerry broke for the third time, again like an explosion, and sunk three balls. This time the nine was on the table, and there were no easy shots. The cue ball was on the table, stuck behind a seven. The two, four, and eight were off the table, and Jerry had to hit the one and had no way to do it. He tried to shoot into the bank and missed the one completely. Under the rules of the version they were playing, if you miss the object ball completely, your opponent gets to pick up the cue ball and place it anywhere on the table to his advantage. Peter strategically placed the cue and with laser-like precision cleared the table and sunk the nine—win number one for Peter. Now the balls were being racked.

There still was silence and tension in the air when the sound of Peter's voice broke through again. He said to Jimmy D, "I've been a Methodist ten minutes, and I'm already a winner."

Then Peter turned toward the table and broke, making the eight ball, and again with laser-like precision he cleared the table and made the nine (win number two for Peter). They were tied two games. Peter stepped up to the table to make for game number five. Peter broke, and nothing went in the pockets. It was Jerry's turn to shoot again. Jerry made one through five and missed on the six. Peter methodically made the seven and eight and left himself an angle shot on the nine (for most players a fairly difficult task). As far as the fans were concerned, it would be a piece of cake for Peter, but there would be no cake tonight. Peter hung the nine up in front of the side pocket—he missed. The fans groaned in disbelief. Jerry was up on his feet, and he neatly sunk the nine.

It was now three games to two, and Jerry was ahead by one game. The balls were racked for game six. Again with a thunderous break he made two balls and was left with a very hard shot. He had sunk the one and the eight on the break and needed to shoot the two, which was hidden behind other balls against the rail. He could hit it, but not make it in any pocket. He gave it a try, missed, and left the table open for Peter. Peter found himself in a similar position: he shot and made contact, but could not sink the ball. It was Jerry's turn again, and he had another difficult shot, but this time he shot the two and proceeded to clear the table. The balls were being racked for game seven. Jerry again stepped up with the same thunderous break, but this time all the balls were left on the table.

It was Peter's turn to shoot. Like the balls were ducks in a gallery, Peter picked them off one at a time. Game seven was history. Jerry was leading four games to three, and the balls were racked for game eight. This time, Peter with a thundering smash made three balls, but the cue ball jumped off the table, making a scratch. Jerry now got the next shot and made short work of the remaining balls. It was now five games to three, and Jerry was breaking for game nine. Jerry broke and again made three balls—the two, four, and eight—and proceeded to run the table.

It was a sad day in Mudville. Jersey Jerry had beat the best. Everyone said that he was lucky and that Peter had played his worst. Even champions have off nights. The two players shook hands to a standing ovation from the fans. Jim and Jersey Jerry disappeared into the crowd. It was about nine o'clock when Dad and Jersey Jerry got back to the house. Dad dumped the contents of a brown paper bag on the kitchen table. It was a mountain of money. Mom put on a pot of coffee. Before the coffee could perk, there was a knock on our front door. I got up and answered it. It was Peter Rabbit, singing and talking in an Irish brogue, which he loved to do. I thought to myself, *What the hell does he got to sing about?*

We walked in to the kitchen where Jersey Jerry and Dad were counting the night's take. Peter said to Jim with an Irish brogue, "James, me boy, is the sun shining upon us?"

Jim laughed and said, "Sit down, you Jew prick, and start counting."

Again with an Irish brogue, Peter answered, "It would be my pleasure, me boy."

As the hustlers counted their booty, they talked about how artfully Peter had gone into the tank and how Jim had engineered the whole thing. Peter was supposed to lose and did. Again Jim took the gamble out of gambling, and no one was the wiser. Now that Peter had lost (at least that's what the public thought), every half-assed pool-shooter in town would be looking to make a name for himself. So over the winter, Peter would accommodate them, playing all comers and taking their money as good hustlers do. He wouldn't need to go out to look for business; they would come to him. Mom poured coffee for everyone while Peter and Jerry talked of the evening's events, complimenting each other on their skills.

Jerry stayed at the house that night, but left early the next morning, and before leaving he thanked Jim for a shitload of fun and one hell of a payday. He graciously thanked my mother for her hospitality and said, pointing at Jim, "There's only one." Then he turned to Jim and said, "Anytime you need me, just give me a call," and Dad walked him outside to his car. They talked for about another ten minutes and shook hands while laughing, and then Jerry got into his car. Jim walked back into the house.

I said to my dad, "Jersey Jerry looked really good. Do you think he could have won on the up and up and beat the Rabbit?"

He answered, "Beat Peter? Jerry's the best I've seen in a long time, but he wouldn't make a pimple on Peter's peter."

I asked, "How good is Peter?"

Jim replied, "As good as he needs to be. When you're a hustler, you never show your speed [never let anyone know how good you are]. I'll tell you this: if Peter was a doctor, no one would die."

Just then, there was a knock on the door. It was Peter, and he came in smiling at the old man and said, "It's a great day to go to the track."

Jim said, "What makes it so fuckin' great?"

Peter replied, "I got my own money. I won't have to borrow from you."

Jim laughed, and they walked inside the house. Jim gave money to my mother for school clothes for the grandkids, and then he gave the bulk of what he had left to her to hold, also keeping a healthy sum for himself. He and Peter were off to spend one of many delightful afternoons at the track.

Bernie's Calling

Now with all this conning, robbing, and stealing in my youth, you would think I'd be affected. But I went to a Catholic grade school in the Richmond section of Philadelphia, and that affected me too. One day, while I was in class, one of our parish priests came around to talk to the boys about becoming a priest. He talked about going into the seminary and giving your life to God. He talked about being a parish priest or a missionary who feeds the hungry and cares for the sick.

I was in the sixth grade, and so far I was unable to read, write, spell, or do arithmetic or remember dates in history, and as far as geography went, I was lucky to find my way to school. You might say I lacked some academic skills. The reason for this was simple: I was a bit hard of hearing, which gave the impression I was not paying attention. I am also dyslexic, and I was dyslexic back in the 1950s, long before it was commonly diagnosed or much was known about it. The dyslexia was misdiagnosed as stupidity and laziness (the fact that I was stupid and lazy or not paying attention had nothing to do with my being dyslexic).

Now we have established that I was stupid, lazy, hard of hearing, and dyslexic. In Catholic school, this got you a lot of ass-kickings and hair-pullings from the sisters of the sacred heart, who appeared more like ninjas in a dress. So when the priest, Father Flatley, gave his talk, I thought I had a calling. What the hell—I couldn't do anything else. Now the church would take anyone. They would have to take me; after all I was one of them. If I were a priest, everyone in the neighborhood would look up to me, and I would get respect. Now here's the best part: the priests were boss over the nuns. No more ass-kickings—hallelujah, praise the Lord! You got clothes, food, a car, and a place to live, and I would have an "in" with God. Oh boy, life is good. I couldn't wait till the school day was over so that I could announce to my family that I was going to make them proud and become a Catholic priest.

At the end of the school day, I ran the two blocks to my house as fast as I could to tell them the good news. I ran in the front door and straight into the kitchen where my mother and father, my uncle Frank, and my aunt Girt were sitting at the kitchen table. (You remember uncle Frank—he was the guy whose leg

I carried around the racetrack.) I said I had something to tell everyone. They stopped their conversation and looked at me.

Jim said, "What is it?"

Basking in my newly found sainthood, I replied, "I'm going to become a priest."

All eyes turned to Jim in disbelief. Jim's son, a priest. A hush fell over the congregation. Then Jim looked at me with a gentle smile and said, "Son, you're spending too much time in the bathroom. Leave your pump gun alone; it's affecting your thinking."

Then my Uncle Frank chimed in: "Bernie, do you want to be celibate?"

I replied, "What's celibate?"

Uncle Frank answered, "You can't get married."

I said, "I know priests can't get married. That's OK."

Then Frank turned his hand upside down and touched his fingers and thumbs at their tops, like Italians do, and shaking his hand at the wrist, he said, "You can't have no nookie." I didn't know what "celibate" meant, but I did know what "no nookie" meant.

My Aunt Girt said, "That's no way to talk to the kid."

Uncle Frank said, "He's got to know what he's doing."

Saint Bernard would have to reflect on his calling. At the time, I had been courting a girl for about six months. We were just kissing innocently then, and I was trying to conjure up the nerve to cop a feel. I was not only a poor student, but also a lousy lover. I had some soul-searching to do, so that night I slept on it, and the next morning, with a clear mind and a pure heart, I went downstairs to the breakfast table to give the family the score. It was celibacy zero, *amore* a thousand. I would look for another line of work. Praise the Lord and Uncle Frank!

The Tapeworm

One night, when I was about twelve or thirteen, before going to bed, I thought I'd have a snack. I walked into the kitchen. My sister Patsy had just peeled an apple. She was going to eat the apple, but not the skins. There seemed to be the same amount of apple on the skins as there was on the apple, so I ate the peels. I wasn't terribly hungry, so this hit the spot. After eating, I called it a night and went upstairs to bed. I slept well and woke up the next morning feeling great, unaware of the events that would take place this day.

I went into the bathroom to shower. Before I got into the shower, nature called, and it wasn't number one; I'm a man, and I would have done that in the shower (just kidding), but for this I needed to sit. When I was through, while wiping, I felt something protruding out. With paper in hand, I reached back, grabbed at it and pulled, and got a sharp pain. This got my attention. I wrapped a towel around me and walked out of the bathroom into my sister's room where there was a full-length mirror. I dropped the towel and bent over to see the problem. I could not see looking from side to side, so I bent all the way down with my head between my knees and looked at the image in the mirror behind me. I saw something about a quarter inch wide and a half an inch long sticking out of my rectum. This scared me, but because I saw my butt, my testicles, my penis and finally my upside-down face in the mirror for a brief second, I started to laugh.

Just then, Jim walked into the room, took one look, and said "Son, you need a hobby." Before he could walk away, I told him of the situation. He told me to bend over. He looked for a few seconds and then yelled to my mother, who was downstairs entertaining my aunts Jean, Clara, and Frances. Dad said, "Mary, come up here and take a look at this." Mom did not come up alone; she brought the whole gaggle. The group appeared at the bedroom door. Jim said, "Bern, bend over and spread your cheeks for your mother." Reluctantly, I did.

Mom said, "It may be a tapeworm." I had several thoughts. One was that I shouldn't worry—because the tapeworm and I were gonna die of embarrassment.

Hearing the word "tapeworm" peaked the curiosity of my aunts. One by one, they walked behind me, bending over to get a peek. When Aunt Clara took her turn, she said, "These things get twenty feet long. Don't touch it; it might go back inside." When I heard this, I became frozen in a bent-over position. After a short discussion, the ladies decided to take me to the hospital.

Jim had left me in the hands of the "yaya sisterhood," who took turns of barking dos and don'ts: "Don't stand up. Do stay bent over. Don't walk fast. Do take small steps." I felt like the women and I were in boot camp. They slowly put on my jeans, t-shirt, and bedroom slippers. I slowly walked out to Aunt Clara's car, with the girls. As we arrived at the car, the girls were discussing whether I should stand or sit. Stand won out. They gently put me in the backseat, and I stood leaning over the front seat. My belt was unbuckled, and the top button of my pants was undone, so my pants kept falling down to half-mast, exposing my teenage ass to the world as we drove to the hospital. I think I broke the Guinness World Record for moon riding. The ride to the hospital included a series of questions and answers about how to cure a tapeworm. There was not one fact-based statement in the bunch, but they meant well. All of these women at some time in my life had changed my diaper and cleaned my bottom, but now at twelve or thirteen, it seemed a long time ago, and each took turns in bringing it up.

Now with my ass pointing at the rearview window and the girls discussing my diaper changes, we finally arrived at the hospital. Now we faced the arduous task of my removal from the backseat of Clara's car. With careful moves and manipulation, I was inside the emergency room. Bent over like a pool-shooter, walking over to the table, with an aunt on each arm, I was whisked into an examining cubicle. Soon a doctor who had been briefed of my problem had me lying over a small bed. He spread my cheeks and called the nurse and told her to hold my cheeks while he examined the problem. At this point, I didn't know what was worse, having a tapeworm or exposing my ass to half the population of Philadelphia.

I could feel the doctor probing, and then was the moment of truth. The doctor had removed something about six inches long. It was red in color. Could this be the tapeworm? If so, where were the nineteen-and-a-half feet? He held it up to the light and said, "Without putting this under a microscope, I would say we've got an...apple peel."

Suddenly, I was no longer in pain, my body was no longer stiff, and I could stand up; it was a miracle. And now the rest of the world was about to learn the truth about the tapeworm—oh no. As embarrassing as this had been so far, I felt like telling the doctor to grease up and take another look. If this was it, why did I have a sharp pain? The doctor's theory was puberty. I had missed pulling out the apple peel and had pulled a hair out of my butt instead. Now the doctor was about to break the news to my mother and grim-faced aunts, who were expecting the worst.

As the doctor explained that it was an apple peel, the tension was released immediately. The ladies roared with laughter. My aunt Clara was the first to compose herself and said, "Hey, Bern, did you eat any seeds? If so, we'll bring you back this spring to have the tree removed." Well, the upside was that I could finally put my pants on, there was nothing wrong, and I could sit down for the ride home.

That night, when Jim got home, he asked, "How did Bern make out at the hospital? What was the problem?"

Clara answered, "Your son's got a hairy ass."

Jim, after hearing the story, walked over to me, rubbed my head, and said, "You take after your mother."

I was never sure what he meant by that, but the girls got a kick out of it.

Billy the Burglar Gets Burgled

One Saturday afternoon, Jim and my uncles Frank and Barney were watching a horse race on TV. After seeing the outcome, Jim and the boys were talking about the winner, critiquing his performance. I can't remember the name of the horse, but while they were having their discussion, the race was about to rerun on video-tape. There was a knock on the back door in the kitchen, just off the den where Jim and his cohorts were huddled around the TV to watch the replay. My mother answered the door. It was Billy Somershoe, one of the East Coast's finest burglars and a flamboyant and very colorful character, always joking. He had an upbeat personality. I can't remember Billy ever being in a bad mood. He also had an ego as big as his reputation. After saying his hellos to my mother and giving her a kiss on the cheek, he walked into the den to join Jim and the boys, and turning his head and looking back over at my mother, he said "Mary, you're a saint; anyone else would have killed this dago years ago."

Mom replied, "He's got nine lives!"

Then Jim chimed in, "Come on in, you simple-looking son of a bitch. Sit down and learn something."

Bill answered, "What the hell can I learn from you?"

Jim said, "How to handicap horses." They were about to replay the race that the boys had just seen, and the phrase "recorded earlier" was not on the screen. Someone coming in at this juncture would think that this was the original race. Jim said, "I know who's going to win this fuckin' thing, and it's too late for me to get a bet in with the bookie."

Billy took the bait; the burglar was about to be burgled. The flamboyant Billy said, "I'll book it." Bill always walked around with a roll of cash as big as he was. He was a commercial burglar who opened mostly safes and vaults, and he was quite good at it and seemed to be always working. Between you and me, hanging around Jim would have kept him busy. Anyway, Bill continued, "How much do you want to bet?"

Jim said, "A thousand on his fuckin' nose."

Bill said, "All right, you dago prick, you got a bet."

139

A second later, the horses were off and running. The word "prerecorded" flashed at the top of the screen. Jim turned Bill's head for a few seconds by verbally jousting. Then the notice disappeared. Then Jim looked at my uncles, made eye contact, and smiled. Jim started to root for his horse, and as Jim would holler for the horse to come on, Bill would hurl insults, saying that the horse was a nag and should be pulling a milk truck.

While Billy was taunting him, Jim said, "If this horse gets in front on the back stretch, he's a winner," knowing full well that's what was going to happen. As the horses rounded the clubhouse turn and were heading down the backstretch, Jim's horse took the lead, just like Jim had "profit-sized." Now my uncles Frank and Barney were rooting for the horse, and with straight faces they yelled and screamed—there were no finer actors (not even on Broadway). As the horses headed for the far turn, the pack caught up to Jim's horse.

Now it was Billy's turn to root. With a smile from ear to ear, as Jim's horse fell into fourth place, Bill said, "Get the G up, you asshole."

Jim said, "They're not to the wire yet."

Bill said, "That fuckin' dog you bet on ain't gonna make it."

Jim, knowing that the horse would take first place again, coming down the home stretch, said in the heat of the moment to Bill, "You want to double the bet, asshole?"

Bill, thinking the horse was fading, said, "Yeah." Now the bet was two thousand dollars, and the odds on the horse were two to one. This meant that my old man was about to make four thousand dollars for watching a rerun. Jim's horse took the lead down the stretch, and the blood drained from Billy's face. For Billy, this was worse than opening a safe and finding it empty.

The race was over, and Jim said to Bill, "Get it up—that's what you get for fuckin' with the master."

Jim's boys were rehashing the race and talking loudly about what a great handicapper Jim was. This kept Bill's eyes on them and not on the TV. He was aggravated at this point. He never did see the "prerecorded" message at the top of the screen. Before the TV could go back live, my uncle Frank changed the channel, saying he wanted to catch a score of a ball game on another channel. Bill took out a bundle and gave Jim his four thousand reluctantly.

Jim said softly, "Like I said, come on in, sit down, and you'll learn something."

Bill answered back loudly, "What the fuck did I learn from you?" He was visibly aggravated, but still smiling.

Jim said, "When you play with the big dogs, you're gonna get bit."

This aggravated Bill more. When you're angry and aggravated, you don't think clearly. Bill said he couldn't hang around; he had to be somewhere. He just wanted to get out of there. Bill walked through the kitchen to the back door, shaking his head, and said to my mother, "Mary, he's either an excellent handicapper or the luckiest son of a bitch in the world," and out the door he went.

After he pulled away in his automobile, Uncle Barney and Uncle Frank shook their heads, laughing, telling Jim, "You got the biggest balls in the world." Jim flipped them each a thousand and kept two for himself.

Uncle Frank called out to the kitchen, "Mary, he's the best."

Mom replied, "Oh yeah, he's a gem all right. I'm so proud of him that I have a bad back from taking bows."

This got Frank and Barney laughing, and the boys went back to watching TV. Jim wasn't the greatest handicapper or even the luckiest guy in the world (well maybe a little of both), but mostly he had big balls and wasn't afraid to use them.

Now, you would think that after this costly lesson, Bill would keep his nose out of Jim's business, but no. A few days later, he walked into the eye of the storm once again. This time, he called the house to make sure that Jim would be home. He wanted to fence some jewelry to Jim. Jim was home and took the call and asked Bill how long it would be before he got there. Bill said that he had a few things to do but that he'd be there in a couple of hours. This gave Jim plenty of time to prepare his next trap.

This time, the trap involved a dreidel, a small toy that resembled a top. It was about four inches high with an octagon configuration, and there was a short cylindrical shaft atop the dreidel that a player would put between his thumb and forefinger to give the dreidel a spin. When the dreidel stopped spinning, it would lie over on one of the eight sides. This would leave an opposite side face-up. On each of the sides, around the circumference, there was writing (on the eight sides were the words "put one," "take one," "put two," "take two," "put three," "take three, "match pot," and "take pot."). This device was used for gambling. Everyone would put fifty dollars in the pot, so if there were four players, there would be two hundred in the pot. It seems innocent enough, but the way Jim's dreidel worked was if you were right-handed, you would spin it clockwise. Jim's dreidel was made so that when spun clockwise, it would always land on "put," never "take." However, if spun counterclockwise, it would always land on "take," never "put."

Billy, being right-handed, was perfect for this game. Now Jim had a couple of hours to get some of his cronies over to the house, show them how the scam worked, and practice playing. So when Bill got to the house, it would look like they were gambling with the dreidel. Jim got three shills from the poolroom: a guy who went by the name of Major, a hustler and candy manufacturer; a guy they called "Ready Freddy" (he had no specialty); and Jim's old buddy Peter Rabbit, pool hustler and racetrack degenerate. Jim made four, and Bill would make five. The trick was to get Bill into the game, but only after Jim bought the hot jewelry and gave Bill cash. If you're thinking what I think you're thinking, you're right. If Jim's plan went well, he would wind up with the jewelry and part, if not all, of his money back.

Sure enough, a couple hours went by, and there was a knock on the back door, and Jim, sitting in the den pretending to gamble, yelled, "Come in!" (said the spider to the fly). Bill, as usual, walked in with a big smile from ear to ear. Jim got up from the table they were playing on and took Bill into the dining room, but not before Bill could ask what was going on, seeing the money on the table. Jim said, "Nothing, just fuckin' around with a little Put and Take."

Bill asked, "How's it work?"

Jim avoided answering by saying, "Let's see what you've got."

Bill went back out to his car and brought in a suitcase with enough jewelry to open up his own store. Bill opened it up and put everything out on the dining room table. Jim, with a jeweler's loop (a magnifying glass), looked over everything carefully, pulling out and putting aside what he was willing to buy and putting the other items back into Bill's suitcase. Then Jim made Bill an offer, and Bill, calling Jim a "cheap dago prick," wanted more. They bickered back and forth and then settled on a price, with Jim telling Bill that Bill had got the best of the deal and that Bill had finally stuck it up this old dago's ass. Jim had a money belt under his shirt, and he counted out a load of hundreds.

Bill was in a good humor. He had just got a great price for his swag, and he had one-upped the master. Jim put what he bought into a satchel and gave it to my mother. Jim and Bill headed back through the den where, once again, Bill was confronted with a big pile of money. The shills were then purposely spinning the dreidel so that they would "put" into the pot, building it up. There was about three thousand dollars in the pot, and all the money in the pot actually belonged to Jim. Bill couldn't resist; he wanted in. They were playing for fifty dollars a roll. Bill's first spin of the dreidel landed and said "put two," which meant he would put one hundred dollars in the pot (two fifties). This went on for about three spins. When Bill's spin landed on "put pot," there was over four thousand dollars, now there would be over eight thousand dollars after Bill put in another four to match the pot. Now the shills were spinning the top counterclockwise so that it would land on "take." A few more spins in, Peter Rabbit landed on "take pot."

This meant he won the eight thousand–plus dollars. The only real loser at this point was Bill, who had contributed over four thousand. Bill stayed this afternoon to contribute eight thousand more. Whatever Jim paid for the jewelry, he had just gotten the bulk of it back. After Bill had finally had enough, he said that my father's house was unlucky. He'd even be afraid to rob it, and as usual, he headed for the back door smiling. The old man paid the shills, and once again, the following day, Peter Rabbit and Jim were off for a relaxing day at the track.

Jim Puts Billy Wise

As time went by, Bill kept hanging around the old man, and Jim finally put him with it (let him make some money and brought him in on some of the scams). Bill marveled at the way Jim's mind worked. You can't hang around Jim too long before he'll let you make some money. Things flowed in a circle but were always coming back to Jim. One day, after a scam that Bill was in on, Bill came out of the house laughing while walking down the driveway. I was walking up, and he said, "I love your old man. He's a pretty bitch. He must get up in the morning, open the window, throw his dick out, and say 'Today I'm gonna fuck the world.'" It was obvious that Bill was no longer a victim, but on the inside of one of the deals the old man had concocted. The mechanics of it wowed him. As he went laughing to his car, it was evident that Jim had another member for life.

The Big Wheel Gets the Grease

In the beginning of this book, I said that Jim made friends with people from all walks of life. He had an innate ability to size up people within minutes of meeting them. He knew what to say and when to say it. This helped him a great deal in his legitimate business: furniture refinishing, cabinet making, and reupholstering. He was tops in his field, and many department stores and furniture retailers gave him work. He also ran a furniture complaint service for stores such as JB Van Sciver, John Wanamaker's, and Bloomingdale's, to name a few.

These stores would deliver furniture to their customers, and if there were any damages resulting from delivery or manufacturing imperfections, the store would give Jim a work order to go out and correct the problem in the home, rather than take the furniture back, refund money, or replace the damaged items. Satisfying these people took talent as a mechanic and the mental ingenuity of a diplomat. Although Jim had many men working for him who went out to the homes and tackled these tasks, often it would take the maestro himself to satisfy the disgruntled customers, or as Jim put it, "ball breakers." These people were headaches for the department heads at the stores, and Jim's service was the aspirin for that headache—and Jim knew that, so his service didn't come cheap.

Once in a while, there would be a meeting of the department heads and Jim would be asked to attend. At these meetings there were suits, ties, and wingtips, except for Jim, who usually showed up in whatever he was wearing at the shop: no suit, no tie, and no wingtips, just paint-stained clothes and shoes. My mother would beg him to get dressed up. The way he looked aggravated my mother to no end, and she was intimidated by the white-collar crowd; she would tell him, "You can't go in there looking like a bum."

The old man would reply, "Stop worrying. These guys wouldn't make a pimple on my ass. Without me they'd be walking into one another." And off he'd go to attend a meeting, and sometimes he would take me along.

On the way to a meeting at John Wanamaker's, I asked Jim, "Why don't you get dressed up like the other guys?"

He said, "When I look like a working stiff, these guys think they're above me, and I'm not a threat. If I dress up and look like them, they may get jealous and look at me as competition. This way, I keep making a shitload of money, they feel like big shots, and everybody's happy."

When we got to the store, I got to witness Jim in action. We weren't in the room a minute into the meeting when it was obvious who was in control. Jim would wind up solving problems that had nothing to do with his furniture business, and Jim would meet them on their level. He had a command of the English language that was second to none. When he spoke, he got right to the point; however, he did add the right blend of street jargon and cuss words to keep it interesting and entertaining. Before these guys knew what hit them, Jim had the meeting moved from the boardroom to the Oak Room (an elegant restaurant located up on the seventh or eighth floor in John Wanamaker's). Everyone was required to wear a jacket, except Jim and me.

Now the meeting turned into Jim entertaining the bosses with stories of ball-breaking customers that kept them in stitches. Then after lunch, the head of the furniture department took Jim down to his office, where he gave him a load of work orders. Jim shook the hand of the top dog, giving him a paw full of money. We left the office and went down to the car. I told Jim I had seen something in his hand. He said, "Being hard-working and being the best at what I do doesn't keep the wheels of business rolling. They need a little grease, and greasing the big wheel will keep the little wheels rolling also, and in the long run, you will use less grease, and it's less involved. Keep it simple."

I said, "You have to give him part of the money you made working? He gets part of your profit?"

Jim smiled and said, "No, when I make out the bills, I overcharge enough to take care of his end, plus a little for my trouble. He's the one that OKs the bills. He's too greedy to look close, and even if he does, who's he gonna complain to? I got him by his executive balls. You see, he's working for me." He rubbed my head, and home we went.

The Spirit of Jim

Now at the age of sixty-four, I think of Jimmy D. and wonder how my life was changed by seeing life from my vantage point. I got an education that you don't get in schools. I never became a master hustler, but no master hustler can hustle me. My head can't be turned by wealth or titles. The importance of having a true friend and being a true friend, not lying to yourself about who you are, knowing how precious family is, and understanding that we all need to be noticed is engrained in me. These are lessons learned.

You'd think this was a strange legacy from a man who ran a legitimate business and was a father and family man while simultaneously stealing for a living. As far as his stealing went, he didn't advertise on TV for business or call people on the phone at dinnertime or load them up with e-mails. He did not go after the honest man. He traveled in the circle of sharks who looked to victimize him. He spent his life swimming in these dangerous waters of people looking to rob, cheat, and swindle him, but he always could turn the tables; he was a master at it. Anyone who has ever bought a car knows what it is to swim with the sharks. Wouldn't you like to turn the tables on those guys just once? You remember how Jim bought his cars: he cut out the middleman. I learned enough from the old man not to trust a smile or a pretty face. This awareness in itself is a pot of gold. But no one travels through life without getting the short end of the stick sometime. Armed with my education from the street, I've been able to cut out 99 percent of the bullshit in my life. This was a hell of an inheritance. Jim said, "You can make it easy, or you can make it hard. Make it easy, and life is a picnic!"

In the summer of 1985, Jimmy D. succumbed to a blood disease that had plagued him for about ten years. He was sixty-nine years of age, and up to his last day, he joked, laughed, and lived every second. The last time I saw my father was two days before he died. He was in his home on Veree Road in Philadelphia. He was standing and leaning on an archway between his living room and the hallway that led to his bedroom. I walked in the house and saw him standing there. He was talking to my mother, who was seated on the sofa. I said "Hi, Mom," and then I looked at my dad and said, "How are you feeling?"

He replied, "A little weak, but OK," and then he smiled at me and said, "Bern, do you know how many suckers I ain't robbed yet? It pisses me off that I gotta die and leave them behind." He smiled and said, "I'm gonna lay down." I think this was his way of getting me ready for the end. Two days later, Jim was gone, but till this day, not forgotten. Whenever family and friends gather, stories about Jim flow freely. People still smile and laugh like he's still around. The memories are still fresh in their minds. His viewing was not solemn or quiet, but alive with laughter as friends, family, and cohorts took turns telling of the escapades that had made up Jim's life. The cars in the funeral procession were too numerous to count. It looked like an endless line of Cadillacs, most compliments of Jim's auto sales (now, he had made it fun buying a car). On the day of the funeral, I saw my mother, sister, brothers, uncles, and aunts cry. These were worldly, tough people. I also saw tough guys, gangsters, and hustlers, especially my uncles Frank and Barney, hug and cry together.

I watched my mother say goodbye to the man with whom she had shared an exciting, fun-filled life that most of us couldn't imagine, wiping the tears away and taking her place as the matriarch, as Father Lyons, known to Jim as "Father Grab-a-Buck," gave a eulogy and in part said, "Today's a good day for the Lord. He gets to meet Jim, and Jim will make him laugh."

When Father Lyons finished the eulogy, people lined up to tell my mother how sorry they were, and each time you could hear them say, "Mary, do you remember the time Jim…" Then they would tell a short story, followed by laughter. After the burial, everyone was invited back to my mother's house. It was a beautiful, sunny day. The grounds around the house, as well as the grounds of the neighbors on both sides, were packed with people, as was the inside of my mother's home. People being on the neighbors' property was OK; the neighbors loved Jim and Mary. And what an eclectic bunch—there were priests, nuns, politicians, whores, mobsters, burglars, gays, lesbians, show-business people, and people of all colors, religions, shapes, and sizes. The human race was well represented. They had all played a part in Jim's life. Now, years later, Mom is ninety and still doesn't take any shit. Jim's spirit still watches over the family, and his memory is still fresh in our minds. Just the mention of his name puts a smile on the face of anyone who had the privilege to know him…There was never a dull moment.

Author Biography

I am a sixty-four-year-old family man, the father of four (three boys and a girl), and the grandfather of four, again three boys and a girl. My wife, Gloria, and I share many hobbies: sailing, golfing, triathlons, and flying. I have a grammar school education. I am dyslexic, and back in the late 1940s and early 1950s, this was thought to be stupidity or laziness, so I went to work with my father, learning the furniture business (refinishing and reupholstering), which later led to my opening a retail store. As a young man I kept an interest in sports. While working with my father, I also played soccer professionally for the Philadelphia Ramblers. I also boxed as an amateur and then professionally in the late 1950s and early 1960s. I've been married three times. My first wife, Loraine, and I had two boys, whom I raised after the divorce from the ages of six and eight. About two years later, I married my second wife, Kelly, with whom I raised our boys to adulthood. She also helped my dyslexia, taught me to read and write, and gave me a new-found self-confidence. After twenty-two years with my best friend and mentor, I lost her to lung cancer. One year later, I met a woman who would become my third wife and new driving force, Gloria. She brought two children (one boy and one girl) and two grandchildren (one boy and one girl) into the mix. Now hers, mine, and ours mix well. I consider myself very fortunate, and Gloria patiently helped this broken-down old athlete write *Never a Dull Moment*.

978-0-595-39485-2
0-595-39485-X

Printed in the United States
57459LVS00005B/349-483